This is a work of fiction. Names, characters, businesses, places, events, locales, and incidents are either the products of the author's imagination or used in a fictitious manner. Any resemblance to actual persons, living or dead, or actual events is purely coincidental.

2

Book cover design by The Book Design House

Garnet and Petunia
The Russians

By

Captain William Gilbert

Other works by William Gilbert

Fiction

Garnet and Petunia The Junior Minister

Garnet and Petunia The Juvenile Delinquent

Pink Taxi

Supertanker Port of Call Cartagena

Supertanker Port of Call Asia

Supertanker Port of Call San Francisco

Supertanker Captain and other stories

The Captain's Daughter

Marie of Gizo and other stories of The Solomons

London Transport Tales of London Life

Australiana

Non fiction

Supertanker Memoirs

Supertanker Circumnavigation

Cuba Port of Call

I

Bangkok

The room was stifling in the summer heat of Bangkok and the white-haired Briton, just on the point of transitioning from middle-age to old age, thrashed around, thinking he was suffocating as the dope wore off and he returned to consciousness. He opened his bleary eyes and found himself looking at the rear of a slim, naked girl who was slipping her scarlet panties up her thin legs, the smooth skin offering no resistance. The man wondered where he was and with whom. Suddenly, the girl seemed to realise he'd come round and spun to face him. He had just a glimpse of something which horrified him and then the panties were covering the genitalia, and he blinked.

The ladyboy smiled and went over to him and bent down and kissed him. "I did good job," she said.

"You did," said someone on the other side of the room. The British man twisted round to see him and found himself looking at a big, thuggish looking white man. The man smiled and went over to the Briton and sat on the side of the bed and forced him to look at some video on his mobile. "Look what you did." He slapped him. "Look! Will your wife be horrified, do you think? Mine would, but in Russia we think your kind are sick." The British man thrashed around again and shrank back, sliding up the bed.

"I don't... I didn't..."

"Ah, but you did." You love your wife?" The British man just looked at him with horror. "You will do what we want." Then the Russian leant in to him and slapped his face twice.

"I will do what you want."

"Good," said the Russian, quietly. "Good.

That's what we want to hear. That's a very Russian answer. You were on that ship years ago. We need your specialist skills just to keep it going a little longer. You will like working with us, once you get used to our style. Total obedience or..." He paused for effect, "Or..." He left it hanging in the air. Then, still with a smile on his face, he jumped up and put his arm around the ladyboy. "We shall leave you alone with your thoughts."

"She won't... I'll explain. I didn't... It's unfair. You doped me up." The Russian paused on his way to the door.

"Once something's been seen, it can't be unseen. You can explain and explain and explain. You'll do what we want?"

The Russian, irritated that he didn't receive an immediate affirmation, turned and then gasped in horror. The ladyboy moving quickly, jumped astride the British man and started pounding at his chest. "He's having a heart attack," she said. She wanted to shout, but years of forcing herself to speak with soft feminine tones made that difficult.

II

Seven days earlier. The Yellow Sea.

The fishermen poked at the bloated thing in the water, fighting the current to bring it alongside their boat. Their yellow teeth were barred in the light of the sodium lamps which swung from the framework over the stern due to their fierce concentration, Eventually, they had it tied up, the ship's boy having leant out from the net draped over the side. Then the skipper climbed over. He spat with distaste and looked up his brother, the mate, who was urging him to make a more thorough examination. The skipper knew this could only bring trouble. There was nothing in it for them. No one would want to know.

The coastguard official to whom he reported it would probably slap him around the face for bringing it to his attention and forcing him to get involved. "We ought..." began his brother, but the skipper indicated with a wave of his hand that he should remain silent. His brother couldn't help himself and went on and on.

"How stupid are you?" said the flustered skipper. "Did our mother give birth to a moron? What place does justice etc. have in our world?" Reluctantly, he pulled out his knife and sliced the rope with which they'd tied up the thing, casting it adrift. "You keep silent," he said to the boy, who was still hanging from the net above him. The boy signified that he would. He only rarely got paid, subsisting only on the scraps of fish the skipper gave him and living, permanently, on the boat and didn't want to jeopardise his precarious existence and he was terrified of the skipper.

The skipper kicked at the thing to send it on its way and then scrambled up. His brother was looking at him with a sulky expression on his round face. "Hah!" said the skipper. "You think you know best. I am the head of the family. I have to think of the family. I do not have the luxury of morality. This never happened. None of us saw anything. Got it?" He slapped his brother's face. The shame of being struck in front of the boy caused a tear to well up in his brother's eye but when the skipper drew back his hand making ready to slap him again, the man blurted out his willingness to go along with him. "Good," said the skipper.

III

Bangkok

Garnet surveyed Smirnov and waited for him to make his proposition. Once it became clear that the

Russian was not going to be hurried, the scorn poured forth.

"So? You want a mild-mannered Englishman to help you draft your nation's apology for MH370, which everyone knows you've got in a hanger in Kazakhstan, with the twenty American intelligence guys who were on board in a local dungeon. No worries, as our Australian friends say. Anyway, we're always inclined to be lenient with Kazakhstan. I believe Tony Blair fired our ambassador who complained about having to deal with their president who was in the habit of boiling his critics in oil. Or was that Turkmenistan, or maybe even Uzbekistan. Hmmm. One of the stans, anyway."

"You're irritating, Garnet."

"Can't touch me, Sasha, I'm a U.K. citizen. MI6 are on my side."

"MI6 hate your guts. That's why they were happy to tell me I could borrow you."

"What's wrong with your own people? Blundering around Salisbury with nerve gas while wearing Russian Army uniforms. I exaggerate for comic effect, but only a little. Why didn't you just arrange a car crash for Mr Skripal and family? That's the way our guys would have done it. When in Rome you know..."

"You're not mild-mannered. People just don't pay you any attention. That's what I want."

"You know why I don't like Russians, apart from Sergey? Because you don't believe foreign laws apply to you even when you are in their originators' jurisdictions. You're a bit like the Americans, like that, aren't you? I don't know why you don't just merge and become one giant, totalitarian state. I believe the cold war was scripted."

"So does every lunatic who can use a computer mouse."

"What do you want, Smirnov?"

"Let's talk somewhere less conspicuous."

"Been at your English dictionary again, Sasha."

"You don't annoy me, Garnet; you just make yourself look like a fool."

"We could go inside." Garnet nodded at the entrance to Hankie Spankie's. "No one in there will pay any attention to our conversation. I can guarantee that. Not your scene, though, is it? You're happily married. There's no filming allowed. Barry the Bulgarian is very strict about that."

"Your third secretary won't like it if you won't co-operate. Gives him more ammunition with your ambassador in his perennial mission to get you kicked out of Bangkok for good."

"O.K., Smivy, you've got me. The one thing which truly frightens me is getting kicked out of Disneyland and having to go home to EastEnders, poor service and strikes. I don't think my lungs could cope without a certain quotient of diesel fumes, anyway. Where to?"

IV

Bangkok

The Russian thug and the doctor looked down at the British man in the converted warehouse that the doctor used for his off-the-books jobs.

"I normally only work on the side for the French Lady," said the Thai. "I don't like this. It widens the circle."

"You could have gone to the States if you wanted to work in safety."

"In my youth, I was a member of the Thai communist party."

"Get on with it." The British man looked up at them, seeking mercy.

"What do you want me to do? He had a serious heart attack."

"I won't say anything," said the victim.

"Yeah, yeah," said the Russian. He turned to

the doctor. "And can he do what I want?"

"Did the French Lady really say you could bring him round here?"

"Doctor, I am not a patient man." The doctor shrugged.

"How do you really feel?" he asked the patient.

"Doctor! I am asking you. I am not asking you to ask him."

"I feel fine," said the British man, wiping sweat from his brow with a limp arm.

"If this job we are doing fails..."

"I won't fail."

"I wasn't speaking to you," said the Russian, furiously. He looked at the doctor.

"It's a risk. Too big a risk, I think." The Russian slumped. "Is he so special?" the doctor continued.

"It would have been convenient, that's all."

"I'm fine," the British man insisted. "I'll do anything you want." The doctor's mobile rang. He sloped off to take the call. When he came back, he stared at the Russian.

"And?"

"I'm required to provide some attention to another patient. Chan gets carried away sometimes. It's difficult to restrain him. Even the French Lady struggles; he doesn't have much of a concept of graduation. You need some more help here?" The Russian looked down at the British man's waxy face.

"I don't think so."

"Hmmm. Well good luck."

"It's time we had some."

V

Bangkok

Ronnie and Angel sat opposite each other at the

kitchen table. Angel was glaring at Ronnie and Ronnie was occasionally meeting her gaze, but, in general, trying to avoid it. "You think I'm stupid?" she finally said. He shifted, uncomfortably. "What's wrong, Ronnie? Seat not soft enough for you?"

"Angel," Ronnie pleaded.

"Don't Angel me." Ronnie sighed.

"This is like a genuine marriage."

"I am getting old, Ronald. And you are ancient. It's only the Bacardi that keeps you going. Do you know that if you dried out your heart wouldn't be strong enough to pump pure, undiluted blood?"

"Be merciful, Angel. I'm ancient. I'm frightened." A tinge appeared beneath the light make-up which Angel was wearing. She leant across the table and slapped his face. He appeared shocked. Thai ladyboys were stronger than they looked. He looked at the floor and reached for his rum and coke. Angel knocked his hand away.

"For once in your life, use your own judgement."

"Easier to cave in to you with some assistance." Angel moved round to his side of the table and put her arm around him. She tilted his jaw so that he had to look up at her.

"I love you, but we can't go on like this. It's time to be brave."

"If only I'd never joined the merchant navy. It all comes down to that." Angel pointed to his glass.

"You are wrong. It all comes down to this." Ronnie slipped his jaw off her palm and looked down at the floor again.

"O.K., Angel. O.K." He smiled.

"Why are you smiling?"

"I'm suddenly happy. You know, I remember, a long time ago, in San Francisco."

"Yeah, yeah, San Francisco."

"My first trip."

"You told me a million times, Ronnie."

"Summer of Love."

"It's always been the Summer of Love for you, Ronnie."

"Not like that. That was special."

"Yeah, well you should have jumped ship."

"I should have. I should have jumped ship." Angel sighed and pushed his rum and coke towards him.

"You made a good decision tonight, Ronnie. Drink your drink and keep smiling." Ronnie sipped his Bacardi and Coke and then, reluctantly, flipped open the cover on his mobile. A voice answered his call. "All right," said Ronnie.

"You're too late," said the voice. "We've got someone else." Ronnie bit his lip and looked up at Angel.

"I'm tired, Angel. I tried."

VI

Phuket

The yacht captain was fuming. His chief steward, Taiwanese Simon, and his mate, James, waited for the explosion. It was not long in coming. "Fifteen years I've run this boat!" spluttered the little man, his paunch being spun from side to side as he twisted to vent his fury, first on one and then on the other. "Johnno!" he said as though he were spitting out poison. "Johnno. A colonial. An Antipodean." James tried to interrupt and the captain went over to him and turned his face up to stare at him. James looked down at him without tilting his head which infuriated the captain even more. "Got something to say Mr University Boy?" he demanded.

Simon wasn't happy about the situation, either. He didn't like to have other people brought into the boat's orbit. He had de facto command of the vessel and wanted things kept that way. The loathsome Johnno was definitely not a good development so far as he was concerned.

"Perhaps we can persuade the owner that we don't need a management company."

"They want to sell him a new boat."

"Of course, hence the offer of three months free management for this boat."

"James?" said the captain. "You have an opinion?"

"I..."

"Ah yes. Thinking about your own career. You see yourself as having a better future by transferring your loyalties to some management company and abandoning me, who kindly offered you a job despite the fact that you had little experience and only a worthless degree in socialism."

"Social Studies."

The accommodation door swung open and there stood the man whom they were all worried about. He looked from one to the other, his suspicious eyes flicking about like a cobra's. You almost expected a forked tongue to flick out of his mouth. He wore the same five-dollar, polyester shirt which he always wore when he was going out on a special occasion i.e. paying for his own food.

"I won't be with you blokes much longer," he said. He smiled. He was one of those thick-skinned people who had no idea how much he was hated.

"Good," said the captain.

"What a shame," said Simon. It was difficult to discern if he were being sarcastic.

"Off to Hong Kong?" said James, cheerfully. "Got to get back to the office."

"A new opportunity has arisen," replied the Australian.

"Another contract in the Pilbara, one hopes," said the captain.

"A new opportunity with another company in the shipping business."

"Good. Seeing as how your current company consists of one Chinese woman with no experience at all of working on any sort of boat and an M.B.A which is completely irrelevant to our business, and yourself and a few others to either look nice or clean the office, I hope we'll soon be rid of your company altogether."

Johnno was affronted. For some reason, he had company loyalty to his current employer, an organisation which was universally regarded as being completely useless. Then he remembered that he was quitting.

Johnno had worked in Papua New Guinea, well outside the just about tolerable environs of Port Moresby, and his bouts of malaria had left him permanently looking sickly and unwell. This combined with the sun during his three-year stint working in Western Australia had left him looking about eighty instead of the fifty-nine he actually was. As soon as he moved, you worried that he might collapse.

He stomped off down the gangway, his knapsack in hand. "Strange," said the captain, in a rare moment of reflection. "Ruby (the M.B.A. girl) never mentioned this. People don't usually resign without giving some notice in this business. Getting jobs in the future is difficult if you've got a record of running out on people. "Hey, Johnno!" he shouted, and the obnoxious Australian stooped and turned round. "What company you going to?"

"Mind your own business." Johnno turned round again and went on his way. "Simon," said the captain.

"Yes."

"Do your thing. Good excuse to get rid of them now. They don't even have a technical manager."

"I don't have the same influence since the Mrs met her unfortunate end." This brought to the minds of the captain and James the photos that had flashed around the world of the Mrs splatted on a concrete pavement in Bangkok in nothing more than a pair of lacy, scarlet panties, breasts revealed in all their glory as, to the sickies delight, she hadn't landed on her front

"Simon, I want a return to the old routine. You run the boat and I spend all my time in Suzie Wong's getting paid to run it." The captain went inside.

"Hmm," said James. "Didn't realise he had that much self-knowledge."

"He just makes out he's stupid. Then no one expects him to work or achieve anything. He's hung onto this boat for fifteen years. You could learn something from him."

James tried to smile but he hated the way that the Taiwanese always made him feel like a disciple sitting at the feet of a Zen master.

VII

Bangkok

Sergei congratulated himself on having given his minders the slip and ordered a pint of Guinness. Alf, the owner of the Union Jack, spent five minutes pouring it out. He cast a sideways glance at Sergey's fidgeting form.

"You know it takes time, Sergey," he said. Sergey smiled and looked at the door.

"Haha," he said. "I have given them the slip." Sergey was another foreigner who was proud of his command of English idioms. Actually, he hadn't given anyone the slip. His minders knew full well where he was and were quite happy to leave him there on the basis that he was unlikely to come to any harm surrounded by a gang of failed Brits working on their hangovers and moaning about their Thai wives, or when they got really maudlin, their former, British, wives. Sergey looked around at the walls at the photos of Lancasters and Spitfires. "Why are there no photos of Soviet military equipment?"

"We're trying to let you know you didn't win

the war all on your own, Sergey," said a customer.

"I like this bar," said Sergey. "No blackies." A retired West Indian bus conductor at the other end of the bar raised an eyebrow,

"He doesn't mean you, Winston," said another customer, slapping him on the back. "You're one of the good ones." Sergey noticed the West Indian and blushed.

"We're very grateful to the glorious Patriotic Army for saving us from the Nazis," said the customer sitting next to Sergey. "And for the Russian linesman's call in nineteen sixty-six."

"Our gift to our wartime comrades."

"We won, fairly and squarely," said another. "I was there. It was definitely over the line."

"You should open up to more Russian customers." A murmur of disgruntlement went around the bar.

"One's more than enough," said Alf. "I quite like it that the Russian Ambassador is often coming in, though. You're welcome. I'm only kidding. Tell you what, Sergey. If Mr Putin visits, you're invited to bring him along. We're still not happy about the old Skripal thing, though."

"There is no evidence that was a Russian operation."

"It was a Russian poison. You can't just go into Boots the Chemists and buy it."

"They were simply tourists who got lost and knocked on the Skripals' door because they heard they spoke Russian and might be able to assist them with directions."

"The party line."

"I prefer to talk about happier things. Where is Garnet?"

"Aha. He's not been in for a while. He doesn't actually live here. He has an office, you know."

"I cannot go to his office and I cannot go to this Hankie Spanky."

"Hankie Spankie's," said the customer sitting next to him.

"Whatever."

VIII

Bangkok Five years earlier

Ronnie leant on the pool cue and fixed his alcoholic's gaze upon the table. To his opponent's irritation, he didn't even appear to be interested in the play, despite his having won every frame; his gaze was just fixed upon the table because he didn't have the energy to look around him. The opponent fluffed his shot and swore. He stood up and glared at Ronnie. "Listen," said Ronnie, "we can 'start over' as you Americans say."

"You're not a charity and I don't need charity." Ronnie shrugged and flopped across the table, lined up his cue, and potted a tricky shot. He was on the table for a while before deliberately fluffing a shot himself because he was bored. The American wasn't deceived by Ronnie's show of irritation. He stared at the floor for a moment and then whipped out some cash and slapped it onto the baize and said, "That's it. I quit. You're good pal. Too good. You shouldn't be playing for money with suckers like me. You'll get into trouble."

Ronnie just looked at the money and then a tiny hand reached out and covered it. He looked up to see a particularly angular ladyboy, who was taller than himself. The ladyboy peeled off a note and handed the rest to him. "That's my commission," she said. "You look terrible so people think you'll play terribly. That's hustling."

"I don't even want to gamble half the time. The opponents insist."

"So, you need a manager." She held out her hand and Ronnie shook it. "Are you retired?"

"Sort of. I was on the pool, then foreign flag, then... I waited for the phone to ring, but it didn't." The ladyboy seemed to be confused.

“What pool?”

“I am a ship’s engineer. Not this kind of pool. The pool was a kind of employment agency”

“How are you so good at pool? What opportunity did you have to play?”

“I never liked commercial sex, especially not with women, so when my shipmates were in the brothels, I was in poolrooms, all over the world. And then at home, snooker halls. This is just a pale imitation. It’s snooker for boys. I don’t know why the Americans make so much of it. The pockets are ginormous.”

Later on, in Angel’s apartment, lying on her sagging bed, they both smoked cigarettes and got to know each other.

“Ronnie, stay.”

“I am staying. I didn’t go back to the hotel. I don’t think I can even find it.”

“Ronnie, stay in Bangkok. There are a million Ronnie’s here and they are all happy. Don’t go home. Who wants you to go home?” Ronnie shrugged.

“My mother?”

“She wants you to be happy, Ronnie. All mothers do, apart from the sick ones.”

“She wants me to be happy with a woman. She wanted grandchildren.

“Not anymore, Ronnie. She won’t care now. She just wants you to be happy, trust me.” Angel whipped the sheet off them and wrapped it around herself, very loosely, and went and stood, looking out at the street action on the soi, through the louvres. “Ronnie, I don’t want a cycle of customers through this bed, anymore. I am getting old. I am twenty-nine. I don’t want to be alone, either, Ronnie.”

“I am happy alone.”

“No, you’re not, or you wouldn’t drink like that and you wouldn’t be trying to get yourself beaten up by ripping people off at pool.”

“O.K.”

“O.K. what?”

“O.K., I’ll stay with you.”

"There's one thing, though, Ronnie." Ronnie laughed, which caused Angel to turn and look at him with surprise.

"You're not going to give me that Mr Sosa speech to Tony Montana, are you?" Angel didn't understand the reference and looked irritated. Ronnie started to explain, but she held up her hand.

"I am the boss," she said. Ronnie laughed, which was still startling even though it was the second time Angel had heard the sound.

"The Frank speech."

"Who are these people?"

"*Scarface*. Never mind. I've always liked having a boss. I never liked being chief engineer. People aren't frightened of me. If you want to be a good chief engineer, people have to be frightened of you."

"Are you frightened of me?"

"Yes, I am."

"Then good. I will be the boss."

"You will. You're kind of like my pension." Angel wrapped herself tighter in the sheet and sat on the edge of the bed. She stroked his thinning hair from his forehead, her hand sliding in the sweat.

You'll buy me a new air-conditioning unit." Ronnie smiled. It was strange. His face had aged terribly, but, by some miracle, his teeth were still in the same condition that they'd been in when he was a bright sixteen-year-old engineer cadet on his first tanker.

"I will."

IX

Thai Coast, outside Bangkok

The shipyard worker took a long look at the stern. Something was haunting him. "I've seen it," he said, quietly. His supervisor wasn't happy with him.

"Something bothering you?" The worker just shrugged, and the supervisor looked at the upper part of the ship's stern in an attempt to discern what had caught the man's eye. The worker turned to him and smiled apologetically.

"I was just wondering," he said.

"Wondering what?"

"Oh, nothing, really." The supervisor considered a reprimand and then thought better of it. He didn't like confrontation and this man was generally an efficient operative. They'd had to poach him from a shipyard in Singapore after the shipyard had poached him from them. Highly trained, specialist welders were always in demand.

The ship was a small tanker, quite old, operating with umpteen dispensations from its flag state, Belize. It'd had some engine problems, beyond the capacity of the ship's staff to fix, and come in for quick repairs. Soon, it would be leaving.

The worker was still looking at the stern. He'd like to be able to climb up there for a more thorough examination, but if his suspicions were true, it'd be risky to be seen to be taking an interest. His curiosity was fighting his survival instincts. "I've seen it," he said to himself again.

He decided to climb up there, not with a view to blowing the whistle, just to satisfy himself. He went round to the gangway and waited for some contractors to drag some engine parts down it and then gingerly went up it and onto the main deck. He saw one of the Chinese crew looking at him and was a little worried, but then the crew member just gave him a friendly smile and he smiled back. He went along the companionway, past the engine room door and then was brought up by a call from behind him.

"What are you doing on board?" another supervisor asked him. "There's no welding going on here today, or anytime for that matter."

"I just wanted to check something, that's all," replied the welder. The supervisor looked at him with confusion and then shrugged and went along to the gangway and down onto the quay and followed the members of his team who were wheeling the parts to the workshop on an old trolley.

The welder continued to the stern and looked over the railings. He was a little relieved at first and then not so. There was something wrong. Ships changed names five or six times during their working lives, even, sometimes, before they were launched. Since the demise of the old European companies which insisted that their ships were maintained like yachts, faded outlines of former names and old weldings which had made repainting some of them, at least, usually, the original, easier were just left undisturbed. So long as the latest name was prominent enough to avoid any fine, everyone was content. So, the welder wasn't too surprised to see the usual mess. Something wasn't right, though.

"Can I help you?" The worker turned to see another one of the Chinese crew standing behind him. The worker smiled to hide his embarrassment and then spoke to fill up the silence.

"I thought it was the same..." then he caught himself. He straightened up and decided it was best just to leave and walked away, out of sight, down the companionway. The Chinese just stared after him.

Johnno came up to his side. "What was that guy doing?" he asked, having seen him when he exited from the engine room.

"He was paying attention to the stern," said the Chinese. Johnno looked even more irritated than he did normally.

"What business is..."

"I don't know." The Chinese didn't like Johnno, having taken no more than the customary millisecond to find him offensive and bullying.

"You do know," said Johnno. The Chinese shrugged, and Johnno went over to the railing and watched the welder walk along the quay. The welder looked up once and found himself being observed, and hurried along. You'd better get a move on, thought Johnno. And don't come back, neither.

X

Bangkok

Garnet went to open his office door and a fur-coated Russian woman tapped him on the shoulder. "I don't do whiteys," he said. "I went native a long time ago." She gave him one of those Russian smiles which means I would like to cut your throat, but I understand this is not the appropriate time.
"Sergey," she said.
"Which Sergey?"
"The Sergey." Garnet stuffed his key back into his cheap slacks and followed her. He was expecting to be taken to a ministerial car, but found himself face to face with the Russian ambassador in a filthy alleyway. Sergey was sucking on a locally-produced cigarette like someone with lung problems sucking on oxygen.
"Sergey Sergovich," said Garnet.
"That was funny once and maybe just a little bit the second and third time." Sergey turned to the woman and said something in Russian and she tottered away on her high heels. "I trust her," he said, without looking at Garnet.
"Nice babushka," said Garnet. "Forties?"
"Forty-one. The young ones are a problem. I like you, Garnet."
"Thank you."
"I like you because you are honest. I live in a world where every single person whom I meet is either lying to me or wants something from me or both."
"I'm British, Sergey. We're not like that."
"Oh, some British are. I used to travel to Harwich a lot. Do you know Harwich?"
"Went to Felixstowe on the container ships a

few times. Supposed to be so much better than the old London docks, with its non-stroppy workers, though they were still pretty stroppy so far as I remember. I know you Russians like to dance around the subject for a while before you come to the point, but we're standing in a dirty alleyway and the smoke from your cheap cigarette is poisoning me. Why don't you smoke cigars?"

"American habit. And I shall look like I consider myself a big man, which is never good."

"You're the Russian ambassador to Thailand."

"Ha! This is nothing, a nothing job."

"Smirnov has all the power, eh?"

"We share the power. Listen. Don't do what Smirnov wants."

"MI6..."

"This third secretary?"

"Him."

"Don't do what Smirnov wants."

"The British will have me kicked out. I don't want to go home, Sergey."

"Ha! No one in Bangkok wants to go home. Not even I. Are you going to listen to me?"

"I..."

"You are a fool, Garnet." Sergey threw the butt on the ground. "My babushka, as you call her, is waiting for me. Can you believe what the court is doing to me over my divorce?"

"You have women's rights in Russia?"

"Worse than in your own country."

"But not gay rights."

"They are sick people."

"Hmmm. Don't you have something on Smirnov to make him leave me alone, a photo of him cradled in the arms of a ladyboy or something?"

"He's a schoolboy. Isn't he a schoolboy?"

"He certainly looks like one."

"Don't do what he wants."

"Sergey..."

"I am wasting my time with you. What is this

word 'stroppy'?

"Obstreperous. It's slang. Use it and British people will be very impressed with your command of English," Sergey smiled.

"Thank you." He shuffled off around the corner in his puffer jacket which had been a freebie from a shipyard in his days as a captain in the Soviet merchant marine, and his tatty jeans and filthy trainers, the combination of which he mistakenly believed made him inconspicuous.

XI

Bangkok

Garnet was sitting in his usual seat at the bar in the Union Jack. The conversation was even more bizarre than normal. An outraged British citizen was reading something in the paper and muttering on and on about circumcision.

"What?" said Garnet.

"If I chop my baby's earlobes off, right, and then say it was for religious reasons, I'll be crucified by the Daily Mail, probably beaten to a pulp in the police station and then sent to jail for twenty years, but if it's a foreskin..." Garnet shook his head to clear it.

"You can't say that," he said.

"I'm not being anti-Muslim."

"And you're not being anti-Jewish either," said a supportive patron.

"What?" said the muttering man.

"You're not being anti-Jewish. They do it, too."

"You can't say you don't approve of circumcision in my bar," said Alf, the proprietor. "I won't have racism. Apart from against Americans or the French, obviously."

"You can't be anti-Jewish and anti-Muslim,

anyway," said the supportive patron. "It's either/ or."

"You're not allowed to mention things like this," said Garnet. "It's illegal."

"That's only in the U.K."

"This bar is British territory," said Alf. There was some rapid Thai between himself and his Thai wife. "You're not allowed to stir up anti-Muslim sentiment in Thailand, either." The muttering man snorted.

"What about the signs in front of bars in Pattaya which say, 'No Arabs'?"

"They don't say that. They say, 'Please respect Islam'."

"Islam is just a euphemism for 'Arabs'."

"A youth what?"

"It's only a euphemism if it's used jocularly and I still say you can't be anti-Jewish and anti-Muslim. It's binary."

"What?" said about three people at once.

"It's binary. Either/or. Like I said."

"What about those non-binary university students?"

"That's sexuality. That's different."

Garnet was wondering if he should find another bar for a while. He was unaccustomed to this. Normally, he was the most offensive customer. The bell on the door tinged and he turned round and saw that it was Petunia come to see him.

"You can't say a transsexual cannot be a woman. That's illegal, too," said someone. "In Britain, anyway."

"Anyone who says that's obviously never been to Thailand." Garnet looked at Petunia with embarrassment.

"They're not talking about you," he said. Petunia smiled. She never took offence at anything. She was, it was generally agreed, the nicest person in their community.

"I hope you've come to put him to work, Petunia," said Alf. "He's been here all afternoon."

"Let's discuss out business elsewhere,

Petunia," said Garnet. "I don't like the company."

"Ha," said Alf. "See you tomorrow.

"I could take my business elsewhere."

"I don't think your three or four Bacardi and Cokes disappearing from the till roll are going to make much of a difference to my profit."

"If it is Bacardi," said Garnet, quietly, as he opened the door."

"That's slander, Garnet."

Outside, Garnet faced Petunia. "Did you find him?" Petunia tilted her slightly angular, ladyboy face and said, "You need to go yourself, Garnet."

"The Thais?"

"They just don't know."

Petunia had arrived on the island on the tourist ferry and immediately started poking around. She had only a snap of a young Smirnov and his much tougher-looking brother, both in Russian naval uniforms, and wanted to make a start. The local police had been wary of her and avoided her questions, deflecting them, changing the conversation, being generally obstructive. In Bangkok and some of the Northern cities their little firm had influence; in the South, they were without any and even Petunia was a foreigner. There was some resistance to the whole idea of ladyboys, too, so close to the Muslim districts. Petunia had been telling Garnet for a while that they should hire their Thai boy on a more permanent basis so they'd have someone available for such trips, but he'd resisted. "Look at the overheads," he'd moaned. The overheads were minimal, but never mind.

Eventually, she'd found that there were others looking for someone missing. A Russian girl had simply disappeared. The family were there: mother, father, brother. The local police were under some pressure from a section at the Russian Embassy in Bangkok. They didn't have time to talk about Smirnov's missing brother, who may not have even visited. "I'm taking a break from the bright lights and going South," the brother had told his and

Alexander's mother, who still lived in a poverty-stricken Ukrainian city on the little the brother sent her and her miniscule government pension, while Alexander lived it up in Moscow, devoting himself to his hottie wife and the care of her own parents, and sent nothing, "Why does he do that?" Garnet had asked Sergey once. "Because he's a bastard," the older man had replied.

No one had shown any sign of having seen Petrov Smirnov until Petunia had given up and sat down on a stool at a beach bar run by a young Brit who presumably had some sort of licence from the local mafia family. "All right, darling?" he'd said, cheerfully. "What's a pretty girl like you doing down here then? Shouldn't you be in the bright lights?" Then, when she stared directly into his eyes, he'd suddenly realised that she was a transsexual. "Aha," he said. "You won't get no business round here. You're just wasting your time."

"I'm not a prostitute," she'd told him.

"Really?" he'd said.

"I'm looking for someone."

"Aren't we all."

"This someone." She flipped the photo out of her handbag. Someone with no training or experience wouldn't have noticed anything, but Petunia caught the flicker in the boy's eye and the slight turning away. "I'm looking for him in a professional capacity. A non-sexual, professional capacity."

"Can't say I've seen him."

"You wouldn't tell me if you had, would you?"

"Why wouldn't I? I've got nothing to hide." He did the open palms thing which sealed it. He definitely knew something. It was strange, too, that he didn't mention the missing girl. An innocent man would have segued straight into that.

Garnet listened to the story.

"Dark, dusky women," said Petunia. "Just the way you like them. You know all the Thais say the women from the South are the most loving."

"I'm a one-woman man," said Garnet.

"Only because you're too mean. Anyway, two women man: Jill and Prudence."

"Prudence is just a dinner companion."

"She'd like to be more." Garnet's eyes opened wide.

"You think so?"

"Garnet, for a detective, you're really useless at "sussing out" women. 'Sussing out' was a phrase Petunia had picked up from a partner from Crawley New Town.

"Well, you don't learn when you join the merchant navy at sixteen and then after getting made redundant from that, spending your time dealing with armed robbers and the like on the Met. But, do you really think so?"

"Focus, Garnet."

"This boy'll open up to me, you think?"

"He's bursting to tell. Just not to a Thai. Give him the 'all Brits together' sense of security and he'll blab." Garnet smiled. Petunia loved her British slang. He resisted the urge to imitate her use of it. She was the only kind person he'd ever met apart from his sainted father, and he didn't want to be unkind himself.

"All right. I'll give it a go. Special Victims?"

"Won't be any help. I did, in a last-ditch attempt, drop our friend's name, but there was no recognition. It's a different world. He won't ring them either. He says it'd be just a waste of time and he'd feel a fool."

"Should I go armed?" This was a joke. Garnet didn't even know how to handle a gun. He was a little disturbed when Petunia didn't smile. "What?" he said.

"Should maybe take a bodyguard."

"Seriously?"

XII

Bangkok

The river cleaners hooked the corpse from their barge and dragged it tight alongside and tied it there. Hauling water-logged corpses on board wasn't a good thing to do. They'd seem some idiot capsize his little skiff trying that once, and they were full of disease anyway.

This one was really bloated. They couldn't be sure, but they thought he was a foreigner. Certainly, the skin still hanging off his skull looked slightly paler than it would on a normal corpse. They chugged up the canal, grateful for the opportunity to cut their shift short. One smiled at the other. They were both thinking the same thing.

On first sight, their immediate superior was not happy. This entailed filling in forms etc., All of which ate into his time with his mistress. Once he noticed that the corpse seemed to be a farang, he was furious. "You couldn't just stick him and hope he sinks?" he asked. "Or at least left it until tomorrow when I am not on?" The bargemen shrugged.

"Just doing our duty," they told him in unison. They gave him the standard Thai smile which could mean anything from 'I love you' to 'I hope you die of cancer'. Their boss spat. Some of the spittle landed on the corpse. "You are contaminating the evidence," said one of the bargees.

"Hah, you think you are funny. There's another barge," said their superior, indicating a smaller vessel, tied up in front of them. They didn't come in today, the dogs. You take that one for the rest of your shift." The bargees scowled. "Go on!" said their superior. "Get moving. I shall deal with this." The bargees shuffled off and onto the other barge."

"We are suffering from post-stress-traumatic-disorder," said one, in a last, desperate attempt to be allowed to slope off for the afternoon.

"Yes, like the American Vietnam Vets," said the other.

"Get moving!" said their superior, and they reluctantly cast off. The boss bit his lip in frustration. Only once before had they found a farang floating. It had gone on all day. The normal police, the special foreigner police, the coroner etc. etc. He hadn't even got his name in the papers so he could mollify his mistress who was furious over his tardiness. He just hoped it wasn't another American. The U.S. Embassy really took this sort of thing seriously. They had no compassion. They'd almost ruined his relationship. Selfish Yankee swine.

The Special Victims detective accompanied the team. Once they'd arrived at the barge, the girl from the coroner's office got to work. It didn't take her long to reach a conclusion. "Already dead when he went into the water," she said. She smiled at the detective. She liked him. He was big and strong and kind-hearted, sometimes.

"Don't you think you're rushing to conclusions?"

"Hah. You think I don't know my job." She smiled when she said this. She still thought she had a chance with him.

"And what led you to this conclusion?" She struggled to turn the corpse over, but couldn't."

"There's a bullet hole in the back of his neck. See?" She was clearly thrusting her fingers up into the corpse.

"All right."

"Look for yourself."

"All right. Don't keep on. I'm sorry I doubted you." He knelt down and pulled at the rope tied around the corpse's middle and when the end came out of the water, he could see it was frayed. "The body swoll up and the force of the buoyancy broke the rope," he said, "with the aid of a few fish. A common mistake. You should use wire. So, they were idiots or they trusted someone they shouldn't have. Can you dig the bullet out?"

"Clean through."

"Great." The detective stuck his fingers into the man's pockets. Nothing.

"Do you think this will go on much longer?" said the barge boss.

"Are you attempting to interfere with a police investigation," said the detective, and the barge boss flushed. "Your mistress will have to wait a while." The barge boss flushed even more. If it were that obvious, maybe even his dim wife would eventually figure it out. The lady coroner laughed at him, and his embarrassment turned into silent fury. "O.K.," said the detective, standing up. He waved the attendants over. "Get him into the truck," he said. "Take him to the morgue. Don't let them cremate him just yet, though. Not until I've had a chance to circulate the photographs.

"You think someone can identify him from that?" said the barge boss, pointing to the ruined face.

"You'd be surprised," said the detective.

Rajesh was getting a hard time in the Union Jack. "Gandhi, don't talk to me about Gandhi," someone was saying to him.

"I didn't mention Gandhi," said Rajesh, quietly, with his usual half-smile.

"I saw a documentary in the nineteen-seventies in which a Bombay businessman said Gandhi ruined the Indian economy," said the ranting individual. "So much for spinning wheels. You don't make a locomotive move with a spinning wheel. And, another thing." Rajesh raised an eyebrow in anticipation. "Went to bed with two eighteen-year-old girls every night to test his ability to resist them."

"That's sort of what I do," said someone else. "It always turns out to be a complete failure, mind; I mean in resistance terms." The ranting man turned on him for making light of his "very serious point".

"I'm not an admirer of Gandhi," said Rajesh."

"So, you shouldn't be," said the ranter. Just then, a lost American walked in. They knew he was an American because he was wearing a baseball cap. Had the baseball cap been a "Make America Great Again" cap, indicating support for Donald Trump whom the habitués of the Union Jack regarded as a staunch supporter of the United Kingdom, he might have been spared his subsequent ordeal.

"Yeah?" said Alf, unpleasantly. The American requested an American brand of beer. "Don't have American beer. Got British, Thai and Australian. Which do you want?" The bemused American told him, and Alf plonked a can and a glass in front of him. The American was looking around him in mystification.

"How about that Tony Blair?" he said, in an attempt to be friendly. "Great guy." The result was reminiscent of that scene in Hammer House of Horror films when the young hero wanders into the village pub and asks who lives in the castle.

"Thanks for the fifty, crappy destroyers, mate," said Alf, leaning in.

"What?" said the American.

"Well worth an empire, they were."

"What destroyers?"

"Aye, what destroyers," said a Northerner, with a sneer. "It's not nice to be so ignorant of something you did to your supposed ally. You stripped our economy." Someone had brought Peter Hitchens "The Phoney Victory" back from the U.K. and it had done the rounds and now the Union Jack's anti-Americanism had risen to boiling point.

"Don't worry," said Rajesh. "They don't like Indians much either. I only get a pass because I'm from a former constituent of the Empire."

"America was a colony," said the American. "Thirteen colonies, actually." He looked around him. "George Washington was the richest man in the country. The Revolutionary War was all about banking." Alf stepped back and reappraised the man. He tapped the can of beer.

"That's on the house," he said.

Garnet decided he'd had enough of listening to this bilge and went out, looking for something to liven him up.

XIII

Bangkok

Garnet sat on the side of the bed in the by-the-hour hotel room in the eaves of Nana Plaza, looking on while Jill skipped into the shower. He heard the pitter patter of the weak stream of water from the broken shower head hitting the shower tray and then Jill emerged and stood in her peculiar leaning motion in front of him, still stark naked. He wondered if she'd developed this pose owing to a woman of her height in Thailand having to lean down to speak to people shorter than her for most of her adult life.

"You always look sad, Garnet," she remarked. He shrugged.

"Believe it or not, I'm quite happy." She smiled benignly. "I'm over the worrying about no kids and no wife and no home bit. That went out on my fortieth birthday. Listen..."

"What?" said Jill, suspiciously. "You don't want to see me anymore because you finally decided to live with that white lady." Garnet looked down.

"You're not supposed to get jealous. That's the advantage of having a relationship with a hooker, or so the online pundits say."

"I don't like it when you call me that." Garnet shrugged. He couldn't bring himself to apologise. That might lead to a genuine relationship.

"I only have dinner with her. How many times do I have to remind you of that?"

"It's a euphemism." He was startled.

"How do you know that word? Most British people don't know it."

"I study."

"Well, don't go using it with the customers in Hankie Pankie's. They'll think you're belittling them and move on." He'd forgotten what he was going to tell her. Then he remembered.

"I'm going away for a little while." Jill made a face.

"To the U.K.?" Garnet laughed.

"No, not to that dump. Down South."

"Singapore."

"Not that far south. Thailand south."

"It's Muslim."

"Some of it is."

"No fun for you."

"Work."

"Some British girl missing?" Garnet smiled.

"There's a Russian girl missing, but I'm not on that. She's not my job, thankfully. Looking for spoilt British girls is bad enough. I don't think I could handle looking for some Russian girl. The foolish things young girls do once they've been on a flight. Judgement goes out of the window." She raised her eyebrows. "It's a metaphor. I know the windows on aeroplanes don't open. At least I think it's a metaphor. It's not a simile. They're the only two literary terms I know."

"Russians are dangerous."

"They do sex better? They never stop going on about it."

"It's like having sex with a bullock."

"Sounds good. What does Britain have? Saps, that's what. Marriageable saps." Jill knelt in front of him and clasped his hands.

"Take me with you, for once." Garnet shrunk back.

"We had that time together in the Mandarin Oriental."

"Barry paid."

"Of course, someone else paid. I can't afford it. I can just about afford a Coke in the Bamboo Bar. Somerset Maugham probably couldn't even afford it anymore were he brought back to life. Listen, it's work. I have to talk to British guys who won't talk to Petunia. They're wary. They won't talk if I'm dragging you around. I have to be their mate and they have to focus on me. No one's going to focus on me with you at my side with your spectacular tits." He looked straight at them. "I still can't believe they're real. I can't believe it's not butter," he added with a smile.

"What?" she demanded, a trace of anger mingled in with the sadness.

"It's an advertisement. In the U.K. On T.V. For margarine or something. I suppose it must be for margarine. There you go. That's what the bloggers are always going on about. Difficult to overcome the cultural differences. You Thai girls don't get the references. It's like having to explain a joke. Well, I suppose it is having to explain a joke."

"Take me to the U.K. I'll be good."

"Hah. I try to check into a hotel with you and the receptionist will call the paedophile squad."

"I'm twenty-three."

"They'll still call them, just to make life difficult for a middle-aged man who's escaped to Thailand and found some olive-skinned beauty when he's supposed to be divorced from some harridan and living in a bedsit."

"Barry says you're bitter."

"Barry's a good judge of character. Never throws me out, though."

"He only throws out drunks and photographers. You're neither."

"My, your English is getting good."

"We could have a baby."

"Half-castes are never accepted in Thailand."

"They are in Bangkok. He could go to the international school."

"You think it'd be a he?"

"Imagine if it's a she. Your daughter would be

a model. Half-white girls get all the modelling jobs." Garnet thought of all the advertising hoardings around town. She could be right. He clasped her hands tightly.

"Jill," he said. "O.K. O.K., but Phuket when I get back, Or Sihanoukville if you want to go somewhere foreign." Her eyes brightened.

"Australia. Gold Coast." Garnet laughed.

"You'll never get a visa in a million years."

"America."

"Even I won't get a visa for there. Have a think. Come up with some more ideas."

"Japan."

"Japan's doable. I'd prefer Sri Lanka. It's kind of like a bit British innit?" Jill stood up and started putting her lacey brassiere on.

"If you won't pay for the whole night, I have to go back. You know that. Barry will be timing me."

"Barry's a git. The favours I've done him."

"He's done you more." Garnet slumped.

"I suppose he has." She finished dressing and bent down and kissed him.

"You're the only one I kiss."

"And you're the only one I kiss," replied Garnet. She left the room, leaving the door ajar, and Garnet sighed and started dressing himself.

No sooner was he outside than Garnet received a call from Andre. Andre, who hailed from one of the slightly nicer ex-colonial countries in southern Africa, the son of a Welsh businessman and his flighty wife who'd left him for home soon after the baby had been born, had been one of the dimmest students in Garnet's initial class at maritime college. To his chagrin, having nursed Andre through his studies, he'd found his friend had gone on from success to success while his own career in the merchant navy had ended with a whimper, and his Metropolitan Police career had ended with a taint of scandal, even if he were wholly innocent of any wrongdoing. Andre had left tankers as soon as he got his ticket, gone off on a jaunt to

Brazil, married some Brazilian beach babe and bought a house on the beach in Bahai, gotten bored with that, moved into some two up two down which his father owned in some miserable Welsh village, ripping down the ivy which had made the place just about bearable, dumped his Brazilian wife there while he went away on much better ships than Garnet had ever gotten, and then chucked it in, gone to college, used his father's contacts in the Freemasons to get a job in maritime insurance and was now living the expatriate high-life in Shanghai, having sent the now morose beach babe home and gone the intellectual route this time, marrying some Chinese lawyer. Garnet wondered what he wanted. Since he'd made the big time, Andre rarely bothered to contact his former friends.

"Long time no hear," he said. "What do you want?"

"That's not a very nice way to greet an old friend."

"You've known I was in Bangkok for years; you've never invited me to Shanghai."

"We just move in different circles. You wouldn't be happy on a trip to…"

"I can cope with dinner parties. I do know which knife and fork to use."

"It's which spoon to use."

"Never mind. What do you want? I'm sure I don't want to help. Some niece disappeared among the bright lights of Bangkok?"

"Not a niece, a ship."

"What?"

"A tanker."

"Sank, I expect."

"Epirb didn't go off."

"Doesn't mean anything. I was third mate on a bulk carrier once. I wanted to test the thing for months. Radio officer was some ex-Royal Corps of Signals hard nut. Wouldn't let me. Soon as he got off, I went up on the monkey island and tested it. It didn't work. Ask the authorities to ask the intelligence agencies."

"Yeah, yeah. The U.S tracks everything. But if they won't tell us where MH370 got to, they're not going to worry about some old tanker with no American crew."

"So, you think it's been stolen. There are people who root out stolen ships."

"They want a percentage."

"No, they don't. I can recommend someone."

"I want you. It disappeared in Yantau, but someone heard a rumour it's been seen around Thailand and, for some reason, its semi-retired British chief was flown out to Bangkok to join it."

"Not interested. I'm sick of ships. I hate those bastards who run shipping companies. They made us all redundant and gave our jobs to Filipinos and Indians. Get a Filipino to look for it."

"This chief engineer who was flown out was British."

"So?"

"I've already told the grieving widow you'll look into it. I say 'grieving' because I think this guy will have disappeared permanently.

"Untell her."

"I've given her your number. You'll get a call. I know you won't turn it down, Garnet. You're soft and sentimental. That's why you didn't make it to captain in the merchant navy and that's why your colleagues in the London police found it so easy to stitch you up."

"How do you know about that? Officially, I just took early retirement. Ah, the old brotherhood. Yeah, yeah. Listen, don't you feel an idiot, hitching up your trouser leg and pledging allegiance to Melqart or whomever it is?"

"I didn't join, Garnet. You only need your father to be in it to give you a leg up. That's all. Then you don't have to join yourself. Anyway, thanks in advance as we like to end our emails to our inferiors." He hung up and Garnet swore. He wondered if the woman would ring. He didn't have long to wait. He was just packing his flight bag in his one-room flat when she called. He listened, patiently. It was the usual litany of complaints that the Foreign Office wasn't interested, the Embassy wasn't interested etc.

"Will you do something, Mr Garnet? I've waited getting on for forty years for him to stay at home with me. He was due to retire in two months." Garnet bit his lip in frustration. "He only joined at the last minute, in Thailand. Someone died."

"I'll look into it," he said. The woman started crying. Jesus, he thought. A seaman's wife who really loves her husband. Don't come across that very often. He said goodbye and hung up. He still thought Andre was a bastard. Andre had no loyalties, no concern for anyone else. Andre was only thinking of his company's profits. Even the worst tanker was worth a few million. Even a handful of payouts like that a year from an insurance company could affect a partner's income.

XIV

Southern Thailand

Garnet got off the boat, following a Scandinavian backpacker girl who weaved her way from the ramp to the hostel, distracting him with her cute ass, which was clad in skimpy bikini bottoms. He tried to put her out of his mind as he walked on past and checked into a guest house, disappointed to find it was full with over-fifties Aussies and Kiwis, the men with absurd topknots in their hair and the women not wearing any make-up in some attempt to demonstrate that they weren't dominated by the requirements of a male-centric world. He wanted to get into it with them but it was essential he kept a low profile.

Petunia had done all the talking with the

Thais and Garnet's mission was a simple one. He waited until the early evening when the sun-worshippers had gone for their nap and things were fairly quiet. He sat down on one of the stools underneath the thatched roof of the beach bar and watched a little lizard clamber up a wooden support. The barman was devoting his attention to an Australian woman who was, absurdly, playing hard-to-get, despite the fact that she was grey-haired and approaching fifty and the barman was about twenty-five. Reluctantly, the young man broke off the conversation and came over to him and said, "Yeah?"

"Singha," said Garnet. He needed to keep a clear head.

"Where you from?" said the young man.

"U.K.?"

"Obviously."

"South London. And you?"

"Lancaster."

"Your milf is looking lost without you."

"She's not a milf. She's a career woman. Stocks and shares. Never had a family and now traipses round the world trying to recapture the youth she threw away. You know the type."

"I do. Fancy coming to Thailand and looking to exploit younger people of the opposite sex Sickening." The barman plonked his Singha down in front of him and stared at him.

"You're with that ladyboy." He flipped Petunia's card onto the bar. Garnet was shocked. "Someone told me you'd probably be along. He recognised her from Bangkok and said you'd be sent down."

"No one sent me down. It's my own company."

"Whoever hired you would insist you came, then."

"Well, they didn't, but they probably would have."

"If I'm seen talking to you, I might be in trouble." Garnet pulled an envelope out of his pocket and slid it across the bar, hidden under his hand. The boy shuffled it into his own pocket. "But I don't care," he concluded. "I knew who you were, straightaway. No one makes intelligent or cynical conversation around here. No one makes any conversation." The young man looked down and then up again. "The Russian girl disappeared. Girls disappear here. Sometimes. Not many."

"Local mafia family?" The boy just smiled. "You?" said Garnet. The boy snorted.

"I have women throwing themselves at me all day long. I don't need to kidnap and murder any."

"That's what you think happened to her?" The boy was quiet. "How about the Russian man? His brother's hired me to find him. Their mother is worried."

"He arrived the day before she disappeared. He disappeared, too. No one is too bothered about a Russian girl disappearing; no one is bothered at all about a Russian man disappearing."

"You think they were together?"

"They were the only Russians on the island. She seemed to have been waiting for him. Put it this way, I made a play for her and I don't usually fail to score." The young man was vain.

"Love?"

"He spent an hour here. Got chatty. Did you know he was on a sister boat to the Kursk? Says the Americans sank it, by accident. That's why Putin had to leave them down there to die and, when they brought it up, they had to leave the bow section behind. It had an American torpedo stuck in it. Bringing it up would have meant going to war. The Russian public would have demanded it."

"Fascinating."

"I love conspiracy theories."

"I can tell. I want to get on. Did he say anything that might help me find him?" The boy was coy.

"Maybe he doesn't want to be found." Garnet nodded at the Australian woman. "Don't you play hard to get as well." The boy smiled.

"O.K., one Brit to another. He did say 'It'll be good to get to sea again'."

"Really? He's unemployed. His brother said he had some kind of dishonourable discharge from the Russian Navy. Couldn't get a job."

"The girl came and got him and took him back to their hut for some hanky panky. He didn't say any more. Listen, is that place still going?"

"Hankie Pankie's? Yeah."

"I hope you find him. Seemed like a nice guy. For a Russian, I mean."

The babushka emerged from the shadows again as Garnet was fumbling for his office key. "Sergey?" he said, mockingly. She gave him that half-smile and he followed her round the corner where he found Sergey lighting a new cigarette from the tip of a nearly expired one.

"You don't listen, Garnet."

"Technically, I'm supposed to take orders from British officialdom, not Russian officialdom."

"Isn't Smirnov a boy?"

"Can I ask something?" Sergey shrugged. "How does he hang onto that hottie wife. She's the sexiest woman in Bangkok, notwithstanding the Thais." Sergey shrugged.

"He doesn't drink. He doesn't get violent."

"And he spends all his time looking for those toy cars for his boy." Sergey inhaled deeply.

"He's just a pussy-licker. Isn't he a pussy-licker?" Garnet's eyes flicked over to the babushka. She still had the half-smile on her face. I wonder if you are too, thought Garnet. "Are you going to take my advice?" said Sergey, rudely.

"I can't afford to annoy our third secretary, again. He hates me. Listen, why don't you get rid of Smirnov if you don't like him?" Sergey frowned. "He has something on you and you have something on him. That's the way Russians work, isn't it? Terror and blackmail. Being kind with Russians gets you nowhere."

"Are you going to listen to me, or not?"

"Not."

"That's it, you're on your own." Sergey swept round and went off down the street towards Soi Cowboy. The babushka shrugged her shoulders and followed him. Garnet stared after them. Russians were not Europeans, he thought. You had to remember that, otherwise all calculations went out of the window. He hoped he hadn't made an enemy. Russians didn't like it when they didn't get their own way. They were like spoiled children, sometimes.

XV

Bangkok

Petunia didn't like cases where her special skills weren't needed. This looked like a purely farang affair. She came into her own once Westerners got mixed up with Thais or the Thai judicial system, when Garnet found himself faced with a door in a brick wall and no key.

She sat demurely at the bar in Crystal's and sipped a glass of Australian Chardonnay. Garnet constantly moaned about Australia's influence in Asia. "For so-called anti-colonials and republicans, they don't show much restraint when it comes to colonising themselves," he routinely complained. That was why Petunia always made a point of drinking Australian wine.

Crystal towered over her and topped up the glass, batting aside Petunia's hand when she tried to cover it. "Sweetie, you raise standards just by being here. How are things in farang world?"

"The same. They go missing; they get arrested; they throw themselves off balconies. Turns out there's nearly always someone back in the U.K. or Europe who did care about them and wants to know what happened, despite what everyone thought."

"They are just worried about the will, Petunia. You need to look at the world more cynically." Crystal looked over at another ladyboy, sitting at the other end of the bar. "Like her." Petunia looked around at the other girl. She vaguely knew her and disapproved of her. She was a scammer. The other ladyboy tipped the rest of her drink down her throat and walked out, leaving the door swinging back and forth behind her.

"I know what you think of her kind, but there's little difference between you," said Crystal. "You both deal in foreign misery."

"I just investigate its causes; I don't create it." Petunia frowned and looked up at Crystal to see if she were being serious.

"I don't mind her coming in. I like a diverse clientele," said Crystal. "But not admirers. This place is just for us." She nodded at the door, "She's been telling me of her latest adventure. Got ten thousand baht just for putting her dick in..."

"I don't need the details."

"You're such a prude, Petunia. Anyway, Whatever. British guy."

"Old guy?"

"Apparently."

"They not usually blackmailable. Their British wives have already left them and their Thai wives never had any high expectations of faithfulness or one hundred per-cent heterosexuality in the first place."

"Some Russians set it up."

"Why would they do that? Was he a diplomat?"

"That would violate the truce." Crystal was referring to the unwritten agreement among the foreign diplomatic community in Bangkok that no personal behaviour would be spied upon or used against people. The consequences were thousands of diplomatic staff happily enjoying themselves in the massage parlours, Go-go clubs and brothels, thus ensuring fun rather than paranoia for everyone. "He was out of it. They had to stick his eyelids open with double-sided sticky tape."

"That's unfair."

"Fair is not in the Russian dictionary. Seriously, they don't even have a word for it."

"Garnet and I could help that guy."

"She's a vicious bitch and with Russians involved..."

"The British third secretary should know about this."

"MI6? They're a joke. They let SVR get on a plane to the U.K., walk through London Airport and murder their own people, and Russians."

"They were probably following them; they probably just didn't know what they were going to do and then by the time they'd done it, it took so long to get approval from the politicians to arrest them that they'd already left the country when it came through. I'd like to help him."

"What did that bitch ever do to you?"

"She gives us a bad name."

"Should get the ladyboy union involved."

"She isn't a member; I'm the secretary for this district."

"Don't get involved, Petunia. Nothing involving Russians ever brought anything but grief."

"It is my profession, after all. I'm supposed to be a detective."

XVI

Bangkok

Petunia took a while to find the ladyboy scammer, following a long trail through cabarets and clubs and by-the-hour rooms. Eventually, she was sat in the same hotel bar as her. The other lady was dressed in high-end fashion which might mean she had an assignation booked at one of the more expensive hotels, possibly this one.

Petunia was still determined to go through with this. She wanted to find the victim. "It's what I do," she kept telling herself. The scammer looked at her and Petunia smiled. The other girl seemed to be thinking and then she smiled back. All Petunia needed to do was to get her talking again and then put all the little pieces of information together. Just the name of the hotel in which it had happened would be enough. "How's business?" she asked.

"Can't complain, and you?"

"Not bad." The scammer looked her up and down.

"Should try dressing a bit sexier. Might get more business."

"Some like the office look. Reminds them of their female bosses when they bend us over."

"I suppose so." The Thai barman wished they were female prostitutes. They at least were more ladylike in their conversation.

"Can I buy you a drink?" said Petunia. The scammer seemed thoughtful.

"O.K.," she said. "Pina colada."

"One pina colada and another martini," said Petunia to the barman, and then she went to the ladies' toilet. Just as she was coming out of the cubicle, the scammer crashed in, grabbed her behind the neck and slammed her face into a mirror.

"I don't want you following me and I don't want you asking questions about me." Petunia, in shock, wiped some blood from her nose.

"I..."

"Don't. Don't try to claim you weren't. You've been asking about me all over town."

"O.K. O.K."

"Who sent you?"

"No one."

"What do you want, Petunia?"

"You know who I am?"

"I do. Don't think you can claim to be a hooker. No Westerner would ever pay for your skinny ass."

"No one paid me. I didn't have much on. I wanted to help your victim."

"What victim?"

"The one you were talking about in Crystal's"

"You weren't there when I mentioned that. Crystal should learn to keep her mouth shut." The scammer stood up and Petunia spun round to face her, her hands gripping the rim of the basin behind her. "Go on, get out. I'm going upstairs to see a very wealthy American and I don't want to see you in the bar when I come down."

Petunia left the ladies, holding her palm to her nose and walked out past the barman, who was shaking his head. There really should be a 'no ladyboys' policy, he thought. "I wish you that woman would stick to using Anglo-Thai hotel," he said. Petunia stopped in her tracks, and then moved on and went out through the revolving door. Had the scammer's big mouth given her away.

XVII

Bangkok

The scammer had found out who sent the thug who'd set up the scene with the old British guy, and stood in front of him when he was on his way home from the Russian Embassy. Smirnov, showing his disdain for anything which reminded him of his poverty-stricken origins in Ukraine, had poured scorn on his wife's desire for a house on the outskirts with a garden in which their kid could play. He insisted on an apartment round the corner from the Embassy.

His expression didn't change as he found his way barred. He recognised the girl, of course, from the photos his operative had taken and his lightening-speed brain immediately deduced the reason for her presence. Confused, the scamming ladyboy felt him mentally undressing her. "You want to discuss this in private?" she said. Smirnov gave her a little smile and signified that he did.

There were a pair of motorcycle taxis at the curb and Smirnov threw his leg over one pillion and whispered into the rider's ear and then turned round. "Follow us, on the other one," he said, sharply, to the girl.

They weaved between traffic, and down derelict side streets until they came to one which was lined with tacky hotels, mainly used by poor Thais in from the country. Smirnov walked into the scruffiest and the girl jumped off her own taxi bike and followed him. He led the way up the stairs, the owner ignoring them, the girl presuming they had some sort of special relationship.

The Russian led them into a room and then turned round and indicated that the girl should close the door behind them. He put his finger to his lips and then went over to her and pulled at the zip on her PVC dress and peeled it down, revealing a flat chest. "I no have," said the girl, indicating chest. You want to pay for some?" She was thinking, this guy is a complete fool. Smirnov caressed her behind through the sheer fabric of her panties and then ripped them off. "Hey!" she protested. "You gonna pay?"

"For panties?"

"For my silence."

"You've never worked with Russians?"

"What's the difference? Anyway, the street says you are one of them pretend Russians."

"I hold Ukrainian and Russian passports," he said, raising his hand to stroke the back of her neck. "You were already paid."

"I want more." Smirnov's soulless, grey-eyed

gaze bored into her.

"And you shall have it." He stepped aside and flung her face down onto the bed and then brutally raped her. At first, the girl struggled, and then she moaned. Smirnov's breathing became heavier and then he swore in Russian as he climaxed. The girl smiled, and then gurgled. His knife had slid across her throat so quickly, she didn't even realise what had happened.

Smirnov withdrew and zipped himself up. "Bitch," he said. For a while, he watched the blood spurting from her neck, staining the off-white sheets, and then he stroked her hair. "Shame," he said. "You were one of the prettier ones."

On his way out, he smiled his rictus smile at the hotel owner. The hotel owner smiled back. Sometimes this farang liked to kill them; sometimes he didn't. Either way, someone would be round later to clean up and pay him. He was looking forward to a long and happy retirement in Chiang Mai.

"She's been found. Denies ever disappearing." Petunia raised her head from her laptop and looked across to Garnet.

"And?" she said.

"On another island. Claims she doesn't know what the fuss is about."

"And Petrov Smirnov?"

"No one's onto that."

"You want me to go?"

"Sorry, Petunia. I don't think she will speak to you."

"So, you will go."

"Ha. You think she will speak to me?" Garnet picked up the phone.

XVIII

Six months earlier, Novorossiysk, Russia

Petrov clutched the receiver of the payphone, his knuckles white, pushing it into his ear. "Don't abandon me, Alexander." There was a snort of derision.

"You couldn't keep your mouth shut, could you?"

"They were going to kill us all, Sasha.

"They weren't. You were just being paranoid. They will kill you now, though. The Losharik., So foolish." Petrov shrugged, stiffly, not like a man who was relaxed.

"I or the Losharik?"

"Both, I suppose."

"It could have been another Chernobyl, Sasha."

"Heroes died. Not you, though. They would have been right to wipe you out, wouldn't they? Someone did talk, you."

"I was drunk."

"Don't bother with that defence."

"You can use me, Alexander. In your scheme"

"You're more trouble than you're worth."

"Alexander, I'm a ship's engineer, a good one."

"Shame you weren't a useless one, then you would never have been on the Losharik in the first place."

"Save me for our mother."

"She might be better off if she were just rid of you, for good. You have a father, Petrov. I didn't want to be your father. It's not my fault that our mother married some idiot and had some idiot son."

"I'll disappear."

"I sometimes need someone. You're right. We take over ships. If the seamen don't co-operate, we can just kill them. If captains don't, we can kill them. Anyone can push a lever backwards and forwards, but when the engineers won't co-operate, it's a problem." Petrov suddenly grew excited.

"Exactly, Alexander. I can do it. I can. Listen, if it's not for family, what is it for?" There was a long silence. "Alexander. Sasha. Are you there?"

"I'm still listening."

"What do you think?"

"And Miss Hotpants."

"Ludmilla?"

"Whom did you think I meant. Of course, Ludmilla."

"Listen, Alexander, just because you married some graduate..."

"If you ever return to her, you'll be picked up. They are not nice to traitors, little brother, even accidental ones."

"I shag around all the time."

"But you always go back to Ludmilla, don't you? I don't know what you see in her. Is it her smile? Is it the acne scars?"

"It's her tits." Petrov chuckled.

"Don't joke with me, Petrov. You know I have no sense of humour."

"Once I'm gone, I'm gone. That's it. I won't care where she is or what she's doing or with whom she's doing it."

"I don't believe you."

"Alexander, for our mother." Alexander bit into the phone chord in the payphone booth he was using in Bangkok.

"Why Petrov? Why do you have to be such an idiot? You never learn."

"Alexander, for our mother. If you don't love our mother, what good is all your success to our family?"

"Someone will get a fake passport to you and flight details to Phuket. Once you arrive, sling the passport into the bin."

"O.K., O.K., Alexander. Thank you."

"You're mine now. You understand?"

"Yeah, yeah, sure."

"And don't go talking. Remember, no government in the world wants the Losharik talked about."

"We were only…"

"Shut up." There was another long silence.

"Thank you, again." Smirnov hung up.

XIX

Southern Thailand

The Russian girl lay on her back in the straw hut, glad that her parents and brother had gone home. They'd only used her disappearance as an excuse for a holiday anyway. She was feeling bitter. Petrov had promised her another life and then abandoned her and left her feeling a fool. She had hot pants but she'd fought her desires and remained loyal to him and for what. When she thought of that barman whom she'd turned down, she could kick herself.

A hand slid over her breast and fingers caressed her nipple which quickly became erect. God, this guy was handsome. He flipped her onto her front and was then over her and as he slid back and forth in her sweat, she felt like she was being smothered in cream. After a few moments, there was a gasp and he flipped off her again and lay looking at the leaf roof. She snuggled up to him.

"It's always better the third time," she said. She giggled. Zander got the impression she didn't giggle often. It sounded a little forced. Zander wondered if there would be any heat from the agency over the modelling job he'd cancelled. But he knew he shouldn't worry about that and should just be grateful to Garnet. The man had got the Taiwanese husband off his back. Since that woman had been splatted all over a Thai pavement, half-naked, her husband, who'd never particularly cared for her anyway but only suffered from wounded pride over her numerous affairs, had been persuaded by Garnet to let him back in, to resume the modelling career he'd been building on the side while working as the mate on the man's yacht, the job title being perhaps more literal than normal, being the mate mostly seeming to involve standing around while the fat little captain berated the entire world.

"I wanted to be a model," Ludmilla moaned. You're too short and your legs are too fat, thought Zander. "You are irresistible to women. Aren't you?" Zander was. It confused other men because they couldn't see anything in him, but women threw themselves at him.

"So, your boyfriend just left you?"

"Upped and went."

"What?"

"Upped and went. This is correct English, isn't it?"

"I suppose it is." It gave him an excuse to have a little laugh, which would put her more at ease, if his lovemaking hadn't already completely relaxed her. He moved his hand between her legs.

"Already?" she said with genuine surprise.

"Soon," he replied. "Why did he up and went?"

"Up and go?"

"Why did he up and go?"

"I don't know. He was frightened. I'd never seen him frightened. He just kept saying, 'I don't want to'."

"Don't want to what?"

"He'd been excited. He'd said he was going back to sea, but then something suddenly changed. Why do you keep asking about him?" Zander smiled and rolled away from her onto his back.

"Just making conversation. I don't want you to think I only wanted you for your body. I saw something special in you. You're a special person."

"Really."

"Truly." Zander liked the word truly. It always

had that ring about it, that emotional authenticity.

"Zander, will you take me with you when you go to Bangkok. You'll be going soon now your shoot on this island has been cancelled, won't you?"

"I suppose I shall." Zander looked at the Rolex Oyster the Taiwanese woman had bought him. It was still only five A.M. No point in calling Garnet yet. He kissed the girl, their tongues fighting each other.

After yet another bout of love-making, the girl fell asleep and Zander went outside the hut and rang Garnet.

"Yeah?"

"Boy was going on about going back to sea."

"I knew that.

"And then he found something else out about the job and became terrified. Well, she said 'frightened', but I owe you big so I like to make it more dramatic."

"That's it?"

"Anything else going on with ships?" Garnet felt stupid. He was supposed to be the detective. Zander turned round to see the girl standing in the doorway to the hut. How much had she heard. He was relieved when she smiled.

"Zander, to whom are you talking?" she asked him. "Some other woman?" she continued with a pout. Zander broke off the call and went over to her.

"My mother," he said. "There's a time difference, you see. She's the only other woman in my life right now." He kissed her and went round her and into the hut, pulling her gently by her wrist.

"Andre, this ship, tell me more."

"Small tanker."

"Yeah, yeah. Crew?"

"Usual. British captain and chief engineer to do all the communications and take the blame and some Chinese."

"And it just disappeared?"

"Yeah, pretty much."

"Search and rescue looked?"

"A token look. No one cares much about a scrap tanker with Chinese crew. Not even the Chinese."

"This captain…"

"Been with the company for years. With B.P. before that. No criminal record. Loyal to his wife. Same with the chief. I've got the company report in front of me."

"What report."

"Things have changed since your day, Garnet. Everyone does positive vetting now. They find out you had some fifteen-year-old in a mud hut up the Congo in nineteen sixty-seven, you don't get the job. The companies know if there's an incident, the authorities go all out to pin it on the captain and anything in his past can be used to paint him as a…"

"Yeah, yeah."

"So, you've got no chance, Garnet."

"Yeah, I'm working for you. You want to give me information or just take cheap shots."

"He's a good captain. No health problems. Unlike the other guy." Garnet was exasperated. He was wondering if Andre was genuinely as dim as he'd deemed him to be at college, after all. He sighed.

"What other guy, Andre?" he said gently.

"The chief engineer sent out to Bangkok. Heart problems. Got his medical, though. You know how it is. Same doctor's been doing their ENG1's for thirty years, wants to be lenient.

"Hmmm."

XX

Bangkok

Smirnov knelt in front of his little boy and helped him line up his cars. The woman who was the boy's mother and Smirnov's wife watched him from their boy's bedroom doorway. She was dressed in that sexy up-market, trophy-wife style, silky, billowing black slacks, a black top which was pretty much lingerie and she had the ridiculously expensive haircut, the cost of which would have supported a Ukrainian village for a month in the old days. She was basically an upmarket, one-client hooker, but the girls in Nana Plaza knew what they were and Smirnov's wife didn't.

"The new house, darling," she said. Smirnov's face normally didn't give anything away, but. as he wasn't looking in her direction, he allowed himself just the slightest flicker of emotion, which resulted in a hardening of his eyes. His boy, whom he was beginning to wonder might not be all that bright, just gave him that usual, gaping-mouthed look. "I so want us all to be able to live together, when you get your transfer home. And how's that going, darling?"

"Soon," he said. He reached out and stroked his boy's hair and the boy purred like a cat. The boy's mother wanted to be serious with Smirnov but had to smile. So unusual to find a man so devoted to his son. Of course, some men became more familiar with them once the boy could talk about drinking and fighting and, to be frank, screwing, but Alexander really was a find. Her father had wanted her to marry someone still in the military; her mother had been frightened of anything connected to the security services, but she had overruled them both and now she was reaping the rewards.

The only thing was his lack of passion. But you couldn't have everything. Passionate men tended to get drunk and fight and get fired from their jobs. The boy leant in and kissed Smirnov on his forehead and she felt a pang of jealousy combined with a tinge of guilt over having felt it. "He needs his rest, darling," she said, and Smirnov reluctantly straightened his back and then rose to his feet. He turned to stare at her and she felt a touch of uneasiness as she saw the eyes go from hard to soft. She knew people were frightened of her husband. At the Russian Embassy's social events some people shied away from him. The only people who liked to be around him were the other wives, to whom he was catnip.

He came over to her and pulled a little jeweller's box out of his suit and presented it to her. She flipped it open. The ring was beautiful. She slid it onto her finger. "And it fits," she said, excitedly.

"Of course," said Smirnov. "I don't leave things to chance." She tilted her face up ready for a kiss, but he disappointed her by only kissing her on her forehead. Still, a diamond ring was a diamond ring. She'd show the other wives at the next do. They got to flirt with him, but she owned him.

"Dinner, darling," she said, and he followed her into the dining room.

XXI

Eight years earlier, Odessa, Ukraine

"I've got something to tell you." Alexander looked at Petrov with deep suspicion. It wasn't going to be any tale of success at high school athletics or in examinations. Petrov was a permanent problem child.

"And?" Petrov shifted with embarrassment. "Don't bother feigning guilt, shame or embarrassment, Petrov. I know all these emotions are foreign to you."

"I'm going to be a father." Alexander sighed.

"One says, 'I'm going to be a father' when one

is happily married. In your situation you say, 'I've been extremely stupid and got a girl pregnant'."

"Then I've been extremely stupid and got a girl pregnant."

"Just marry Ludmilla. I'm sick of you mooning over her. Just marry her and be done with it." Petrov looked genuinely embarrassed. "What's the problem?"

"It's not Ludmilla?" Alexander considered this.

"Who then?" Petrov disclosed that it was the daughter of a local political bigwig. "Marry her, then."

"I can't. I'm in love with Ludmilla."

"The father won't stand for this, you know."

"That's why I need big brother."

"And what do you want me to do?"

"What's the point in having a big brother in the security services if he can't sort out something like this for his own family?"

"I'm only a junior official. He's senior."

"Yeah, in local politics. Big deal. Mother won't like it if you leave me hanging in the wind."

"Why did she ever marry your idiot father? I can't believe it. I couldn't believe it then. Even though I was only ten, I knew him to be a fool."

Alexander saw the father of the pregnant girl, who screamed at him while chugging vodka, working himself up into a greater and greater rage. "My brother is an idiot," said Alexander. "Do you really want him for a son-in-law?" The father considered this and affirmed that he did. "Well, you can't have him." The man raised himself up from his armchair. "Sit down," said Alexander calmly. "His military service is coming up. I'm arranging that he goes into the navy. He'd come to harm in the army and he hasn't the brains for the air force. He'll be sent away. He won't be around." He flicked a business card at him. "This is an abortion clinic, masquerading as a beautician's. It's approved, semi-officially, by the authorities. The fee's already paid. If you want to kill your grandson or granddaughter, go ahead, but my brother is not going to be the baby's father. I'm just a junior now, but I'll rise and it's better to have someone in the security services on your side than against you, don't you think?"

"I don't want to go on submarines," said Petrov, later that afternoon. "Can you keep me off them?"

"I can't. Just do your service, Petrov."

"I'm claustrophobic."

"Do you know what they do to recruits who claim this? They lock them up in a coffin-size box without a light for twenty-four hours to verify it. If you're completely insane when you're released, then they accept that you're claustrophobic. If you're not, then you're not. Don't like the sound of that? Then don't make any false claims."

"I want to marry Ludmilla."

"You're not marrying Ludmilla. You've caused that man enough shame as it is. If you go and marry some other girl, he'll explode, your family being involved with the security services being forgotten in his fury. Anyway, she's even more stupid than you; she's a little whore and she's only fifteen."

"You're cruel, Alexander."

"I'm practical, not a dreamy, romantic idiot. Just hope that that man gets himself arrested for corruption or something soon and I can bail him out and gain the moral higher ground."

"Mother will be happy with me in uniform," said Petrov with a smile.

"She loves her little boy," confirmed Alexander. "I don't know why. I am the success; you are a permanent failure, a disaster."

"I'm the kind-hearted one."

"That's just polite for the foolish one."

XXII

Bangkok

Garnet and Prudence sat, once again, in the Argentinian steak restaurant. "This comes from Argentina," said the proprietor, leaning in to them. "Not from Australia like normal."

"Should do for the price," said Garnet. Prudence made to playfully slap him.

"I'm paying, Garnet, don't be rude," she said. He didn't smile, and the proprietor disappeared to welcome some Hi So Thais.

"I'm a kept man."

"Kept men do a bit more for their keep than you. How's Jill?"

"Why is it that women on a date always want to talk about the other women in their men's lives."

"Just a thought, Garnet. You won't ever talk about your work."

"It's just so sleazy. I'd like to be able to make some Hollywood cop's speech about how terrible the sights I see are, but they're not terrible; they're just sleazy and pathetic."

"Sleaze can be fun."

"Not Ann Summers'-style sleazy.

"I don't wear Anne Summers. Is there a shop here anyway?"

"Vitoria's Secret?" said Garnet with a little smile.

"You think I'm a Marks and Spencer woman don't you. I wouldn't be offended. I am."

"The nice middle-class girl at the back of the class."

"I'd wear Victoria's Secret for you, Garnet."

"Garnet suddenly looked frightened, and Prudence laughed.

"Ha," she said. "Don't know what to do, do you? Only women you normally speak to are your victims and Thai dancers."

"What do you mean victims?"

"Those distraught mothers whom you rob in the Bamboo bar at the Mandarin Oriental when they come looking for their little darlings. Does that hotel know you're running a business out of there?"

"I'm not running a business. I have meetings, that's all."

"Garnet, I'm lonely. I finally realized that I will never have a child, and that I don't want one."

"Buy a Pekingese."

"Dog or person?"

"Hah. That's funny." Garnet looked around him. "As long as there's no Chinese listening." He tried to avoid her eyes by taking a long time to saw a piece of steak. "I'm not the marrying kind."

"I know that. It doesn't bother me."

"I swim in the sewers, Prudence."

"Ah, the old 'You're too good for me' line."

"It's no line in this case. You really are too good for me."

"Don't you think I'd like some fun, sometimes."

"I invite you to Hankie Spankie's."

"Naked women dancing."

"White women come in. Baz doesn't like it, but he lets them in sometimes."

"Garnet."

"I don't approve of them, myself, now I come to think of it."

"Garnet, stop avoiding the question."

"What was the question? I'm confused."

"No, you're not."

"I don't want to give up my freedom."

"Freedom to do what? All right. We can just be f**k buddies." Garnet was genuinely shocked. Prudence reddened, but still smiled at him.

"If it doesn't work out, it'll ruin our relationship."

"At the moment, we're just dinner partners. There's not all that much to ruin."

"Ruthless women's logic.

"So, you'll think about it." Garnet scoffed.

"If I think about it, we'll never get round to it. Let's skip dessert." Garnet felt a pang of remorse but then rationalised things. How could he be betraying Jill when she'd probably had some fat sex tourist slamming into her while they were dining.

XXIII

Bangkok

Garnet swung his swivel chair from side to side and chewed on his red pen. Writing everything in red ink was a fetish of his and he could never understand why it always wound everyone up. He slapped the pen down on his pad. "Anglo Thai," he said. Petunia just looked at him. Her face was a little bruised, but, thankfully, her nose wasn't broken and her skin wasn't cut. Maybe it's a mis translation. Anglo Siamese?"

"Possibly, Garnet."

"It's an odd one. That's not a known hotel either. Hookers don't use third-rate hotels which no one has even heard of. I can't even find it."

"I tried Special Victims. They don't know of it. Some hotels don't even have names, or they don't have English versions."

"But why Anglo-Thai."

Later on, Garnet was in the Union Jack. "Who ever heard of the Anglo Siamese hotel?" he asked. There was silence and Garnet looked at his Guinness beer mat morosely.

"You're a seaman and you don't remember the Anglo-Siamese?" said someone. Garnet looked up. It was an old Scot who'd been in the merchant navy in the good old days before containerisation, the sweeping out of the old owning families by the chinless wonders in the City of London, and the stupid regulation of the hated International Maritime Organisation, had ruined it. "And you're best mates with Ronnie."

"What's Ronnie got to do with it?" asked Garnet with a raised eyebrow.

"We were often there in the seventies. The hotel on the original site was built for other ranks. The captains and the diplomats had the original Oriental. When they put up the concrete monstrosity which replaced the Anglo Siamese some people kept using the name. You know, like how the captains on the Thames insist on using the name of some pub which was demolished years ago when they report in, instead of using the official name of the station."

"They only do that to confuse all the foreigners on the river."

"Yeah, but you get my point."

"And the new name." The Scot told him.

"I think that entitles you a drink. MacEwan's for my good friend," Garnet said to Alf. The publican pulled a can out of the fridge.

"Where is Ronnie?" said the old chief engineer.

"Hangs out at that ladyboy pool joint," said someone who'd remained silent for a while.

"When you going to get a pool table, Alf?" asked someone else.

"When you going to get ladyboys?" said yet another person. Alf made a face.

"Wife won't let me. Thinks I'll go on the turn." He paused and looked around at all his grinning customers. "Like the rest of you," he said. There was a general shuffling and a lot of blushes. "Hah," said Alf. "Don't worry, you lot, your secret's safe with me."

"I'm all right," said Garnet, cheerfully, "I'm in love with Jill."

"You're in love with Petunia, Garnet. The whole world knows this, apart from you." Someone giggled. Garnet flushed redder than any of them.

XXIV

Six months ago, Bangkok

Garnet was swooping through Nana Plaza, looking for business and had Ronnie in tow, whom he'd salvaged from the floor of some bar near the entrance. To anyone who didn't know him, Ronnie would just appear to be lost, but to those who did know him, there were some telltale signs as to his true state. Years of being at sea had taught him to remain upright even under the most difficult circumstances, but there were other indications. His yellowy eyes were slightly glazed and he had a weird grin upon his face. "Angel," he said.

"Never mind Angel, Ronald. Angel's working," replied Garnet. "Well, well, look who it is." Smirnov stood before them, his face impassive, as per usual.

"Garnet," said Smirnov. His rictus smile appeared.

"What you doing in this den of sin?" Smirnov. "Upon whom are you spying? Hankie Pankie's is full with your countrymen, but they don't seem to be the sinister types, more like the jovial style of Russian, the sort not worth spying on. You could join them, but I don't expect they'll enjoy your company or you will enjoy theirs." Smirnov looked at Ronnie. "Allow me to perform the introductions," said Garnet. "This is Ronnie, AKA Skinny Ronald, best pool player among the expatriates in Bangkok, with the possible exception of Fat Les, and the most brilliant marine mechanic in the history of steam navigation."

"Don't have a steam ticket," said Ronnie.

"Diesel navigation."

"Heavy fuel oil navigation and it's engineer, not mechanic, if you don't mind."

"I do not mind, Ronald. Most brilliant engineer in the history of heavy fuel oil navigation, Sasha." Smirnov's eyes bored into Ronnie's as a cobra's would into a rat's.

"That's good to know," he said.

"Never went to sea, did you Smivy, not even when you were in the Russian navy. Exempt from service due to your being a trainee torturer of the people."

"It's always nice to reacquaint myself with Britain's finest specimens," said Smirnov.

"Join us for a drink," said Ronnie. Garnet hissed.

"You've had enough, Ronniepoos. Ronnie has good contacts in the transsexual world, Sasha. Not into that, though, are you? Hottest wifey in the community."

"It's not polite to comment upon other people's wives," interjected Ronald, "either positively or negatively."

"You should listen to him, Garnet."

"Come down the pool hall, Mr Smirnov. I shall teach you to play. Consider it an attempt at reparations to Anglo-Soviet relations. I'm assuming, of course, that my good friend, Mr Garnet, has just trashed them."

"They're not Soviets anymore, Ronnie, they're a mafia. I do wish you would make more of an effort to keep up with the news. It's been thirty years. Surely you could have found the time to update yourself a little." Smirnov's smile broadened.

"Gentlemen, it's been a pleasure, but I must be moving on. Good day to you both." He held out his hand. Garnet shook it reluctantly, and Ronnie, enthusiastically. He walked round them and they turned to watch him go.

"Don't like him," said Garnet.

"Seems nice enough to me," replied Ronald. "Remember what they told us at navigation school, or in my case, marine engineering school: only Russian and American ships carry doctors these days and if you're sick or you've got someone sick, contact a Russian ship, don't bother with the Americans; they'll just tell you to shove off."

"I got smashed with some in Ulsan once. They were great guys. Kept tipping vodka down my throat and forcing me to smoke their sickening cigarettes. Wouldn't let me pay. They were probably only on subsistence wages. He's a bad 'un though."

"Can't judge them all on the basis of a sample of one. Look at our third secretary. He's nothing like the rest of us."

"Thank God. One of him is more than enough." They went on their way.

XXV

Southern Thailand

The Russian girl moped around on the island. The British boy had just disappeared. They'd woken up together and he'd said to her "ships that pass in the night" and then he was gone. Why did he mention ships, she wondered until some other British guy told her it was just a phrase.

She missed Petrov. She'd turned down that barman on the other island for him. They'd been sweethearts since school. She'd waited for him throughout his time in the Navy, distraught after the Kursk, wondering if his submarine would be next. There was just that one time with the friend of her father's, but she justified that. He was so old that their fling was obviously just a physical necessity for her and couldn't be interpreted as an emotional betrayal.

The sea breeze blew her long hair into her eyes as she strolled along the sand and she flicked it out only to have it get in them again. She grabbed it and tied it in a topknot and looked out at a tanker in the distance.

Petrov, she thought, why did you have to be such a romantic. You could have got a job like your brother's, as an enforcer for the mob which happened to have won the race to obtain political power, in the SVR, security. All those special privileges. And you're always complaining and telling everyone your crazy theories. Americans don't torpedo Russian submarines anymore, Petrov.

Two local boys, crouching in the sand, gave her the eye. It amused her to remember all the fuss when she'd disappeared. They thought she'd been raped and murdered. Her parents went mad, completely crazy. And her brother. He spent his whole life reading books about the Great Patriotic War, yet had been rejected for military service, being judged too feeble. So, he made up for it, lecturing her on all the worry she had caused their parents.

Oh, Petrov, she thought. You said you would take me with you and you didn't.

"All right, darling?" She looked behind her and there was another British youth standing there, his six pack on display, a can of lager in his hand even though it was only eight O'clock in the morning. She wondered why the only British males whom you ever saw were either fit teenagers and twenty-somethings with six packs or beer-bellied, middle-aged baldies. What happened to them. Little did she know that the British men wondered why you only ever saw sweet, svelte, teen Russian girls or hatchet-faced, plump babushkas and never anything in between.

"I am married," she said to get rid of him.

"No, you're not," he replied.

"Excuse me," she said.

"No, you're not. You're just lost. The beach bar is open for breakfast."

"I don't want your disgusting British breakfast."

"They do a kind of continental thing. Fruit and all that."

"Thank you for the information."

"Come on then."

"You are very rude." The boy shrugged.

"Why shouldn't I try it on. It's not like you're from my hometown. We're never going to see each other again once we leave this island, are we?" The girl was surprised that this Russian-style logic came from a British guy and one who didn't seem particularly intelligent at that. The boy shrugged and turned to go.

"Wait," she said. She bit her lip and walked up to him.

"Preferred you with your hair down."

"So, you've been spying on me."

"I'm just observant and I have a good memory."

"It gets in my eyes."

"Some sacrifices have to be made for beauty. Full English on me. Live a little." The boy smiled as he traipsed along, the girl at his side. That other English guy, the one who wore his sunglasses as if he were in a commercial, had nailed her after half an hour's conversation in the Tiki Hut. This shouldn't be too difficult.

XXVI

Bangkok

Petunia hung around in the lobby of the former Anglo-Siamese, waiting for two Filipino seamen to complete check in. They didn't want to hand their passports over, but the owner insisted. They dragged their bags over to the lifts. "Elevator not working," said the owner.

"But our rooms are on the sixth floor," protested one of the seamen in his sing-song accent. The owner just shrugged and the Filipino looked to his companion and then gave a resigned sigh and dragged his suitcase over to the bottom of the stairs. Petunia walked over to the desk.

The owner looked her up and down. "Only ladyboys with arrangement operate in here," he said. "You want to make arrangement?"

"I'm not a prostitute."

"You wouldn't get much business in that outfit anyway. Plus, you need operation. Seamen miss their mothers. They like big tits." Petunia thought the man was revolting and, unfortunately, he could see the revulsion on her face. "Out, go on," he said. "Leave!"

"I don't think I will." The owner had turned back to his receipts, but now he looked up at Petunia with mystification on his face.

"What?"

"I don't think I will." She looked around her. "This place is a real dump. I bet it was elegant when it was the Anglo-Siamese. Pot plants, uniformed bell-boys. That type of thing. That was when you had European seamen, though, wasn't it, and Americans. Now you have Somalis, Filipinos, Pakistanis. Their companies don't care about them." She looked at the owner again and smiled. "You know who I am? I'm the top detective in Bangkok. Well, my boss thinks he is the top detective, but, in reality, I am."

"Where's your I.D. card?"

"I'm not official; I'm private."

"So, you have no authority. Get out."

"There have been complaints about this hotel. I checked with the Filipino consulate. Some of their seamen weren't too embarrassed to file them. But never mind them. I think you know whom I'm interested in."

"I haven't seen any police," said the owner, with a sneer.

"Do you want to?"

"Eh?"

"Do you want to see some in your establishment? You know what? I'm wasting my time." She mentioned the name of her feared associate in Special Victims and smiled. "Yes," she said. "You're quite right. This is definitely a job for officialdom. You, being a respected businessman, should only be dealing with the proper authorities."

"Wait," said the man. Petunia raised an inked-on eyebrow. "What do you want?"

"Something went on with a British seaman. Can't you take a hint."

"Be more specific." Petunia gave him a wry smile.

"So, there've been more than one." She paused for effect. "Something recent."

"If I tell you…"

"When you tell me."

"Some pimp and a scammer. I don't know their names."

"I Know her name already. I want his name."

"And I told you that I don't know."

"I'm wasting my time with you." Petunia flipped open the cover on her mobile.

"Wait." He gave her the name and claimed he didn't know anymore." She turned to go. The foolish man giggled.

"Something funny?"

"You could be a hooker, you know. You'd appeal to those farang businessmen in the expensive hotels. They like to imagine they're doing their lady bosses."

"Someone else said something similar. I take it as a compliment. This isn't over."

XXVII

Southern Thailand

The British boy woke up and found his head hurt, and it felt as if he were lying in a little pool of water. With an effort, he sat up and realised his shirt was more damp than it should have been if the only cause were sweat. He squinted in the light which came through the gap in the bamboo doors of the hut and wiped his face and stared at his hand. It was covered in blood.

With a touch of dizziness, he rose to his feet and tramped along the sand until he came to the beach bar. Slumping down onto a stool, he stared at the menu and failed to hear the boy who was serving. Eventually, he looked up into the brown face. "You O.K.? said the Thai, and then the British boy slid off the stool and lay on his side in the sand.

He came round when the boy and the cook had hauled him into a sitting position. Now he remembered something. Shouting in Russian and then... The cook spoke sharply to his boy and the boy ran off. Five minutes later, he came back with Big Gay Bob, the owner, in tow, while he continued to squeak excitedly.

"I can hear you; I can hear you," said the big man in a Californian accent. His belly wobbled from side to side, his too-tight singlet doing little to restrain its movement. Once they had arrived, he looked down at the British boy. "Fight?" he said.

"I woke up like this." There was some rapid Thai.

"Russians," said Big Gay Bob. "I try to keep them off the island, I don't own the huts. She would never have been staying there if I did." Bob had been brought up during the Cold War and loathed Russians. Personally, he would never understand why Uncle Sam hadn't nuked their country while they were still in the business of torturing their own captured German scientists in a bid to get them to speed up production of their own bomb. "Got any medical insurance?" The British boy shook his head.

"Guess, you're screwed then." He bent down and had a look at the boy's scalp. "Only kidding. I was a medic in the U.S.N. I can stitch that up."

"I still don't know what happened."

"You messed with someone else's woman, son." A teenage Thai boy in a singlet and too-short, satin shorts came trotting up. "Come on," said Bob, still looking at the British boy. "Let's get you to my place and I'll get stitching." He hauled the victim up and put the boy's arm around his own shoulder. His boyfriend tried to help but Bob just waved him away. "I'm still fit," he said. They went wobbling across the sand.

"But what happened?" insisted the British boy.

"According to my staff, that hotpants, Russian bitch's boyfriend came in on a little boat, went into the girl's hut, and she came out with him and they were gone. My people had no idea he'd beaten you up or they would have alerted me.

"And?"

"I'd have brought the police round."

"And?"

"Oh, they would have done something. They don't like Russians, either, even though the Brits cause them far more work. I hope she was worth it, son."

"I don't know."

"Should go gay. Try it. Don't write it off until you've seen what it can do for you."

"You're not going to rape me, are you?" They both laughed, but the British boy's laugh had a nervous quality about it.

XXVIII

Bangkok

The skinny man slipped away from the wall in the basement room, tired of listening to the long laments and the hate-filled rants. His target had moved away from his little circle and was standing on his own, lighting up a Marlboro. He didn't look at the skinny man as he approached him, but a slight smile came onto his face. His diamond-like eyes focussed on his lighter and then turned to him.

"And?" he said. The skinny man smiled at the patrician face and took in the hundred-dollar haircut, the thirty-thousand-dollar smile, the absence of the stress lines which you normally found on men in their fifties. The man's voice was reassuring, just the kind of voice which relaxed institutional shareholders at companies' yearly shareholders meetings on Wall Street.

"Got something, that's all," said the skinny man.

"You Brits are always so vague. You approached me; I didn't approach you. Don't flirt with me." The skinny man looked a little offended, but the American was right: he was a seller, not a buyer. "So? Where? In the City?"

"Will be soon."

"So, this is putative." The skinny man hadn't learnt this word at his inner-city, British comprehensive. "I mean, it is something which might happen?"

"Oh, it will happen, all right."

"And why would I be interested?"

"I just thought."

"I did business with you once; I wasn't particularly impressed."

"It'll be better this time." The American took a long puff on his cigarette.

"You know, a big reason why I like this country is that you can smoke indoors, at least unofficially. And, of course, the other... American?"

"That's a bit too much to expect, isn't it?

"It's a buyer's market."

"It's a seller's market." The American looked annoyed.

"I'm rapidly losing interest. Don't tell me it's a Brit."

"That's not very... American, referring to a woman as 'it'?"

"Yeah? Why don't you 'run along' as you Brits say."

"Russian."

"Probably some kind of ethnic Russian. Not interested."

"St Petersburg, Leningrad to you commie-haters."

"I'm beginning to build a mild curiosity. Nothing more."

"You're not the only buyer in town."

"True. Try to find another. Good luck."

"O.K., O.K. Believe me, it'll be worth it. She's fluent in English." The American businessman raised an eyebrow.

"That's interesting."

"And not a hooker." The American took another puff.

"That's even more interesting. I tire of the soulless."

"So, can we do a deal?"

"Don't bother me until the product's in stock." The skinny man shifted, uncomfortably.

"I might need to put down a deposit.

"Fat chance of getting that from me."

"Come on. A foreigner. A white girl."

"It's not such a big deal. Some rural county back home, I can obtain the same, probably cheaper."

"But you're not back home. And Russian? A clean one. University girl. Not some crack-addicted runaway."

"It's all OxyContin now. Do your research, boy."

"So, you'll think about it."

"O.K. If the only way to get rid of you is to tell you I'll think about it, I'll think about it."

"And the deposit. I need…"

"I just told you, didn't I, that I'll think about it."

"Cool. I just wanted to know. That's all. The skinny man backed away and melted into the seething mass, whose emotions were being stirred and whose tempers were being raised to boiling point by a sobbing plaintive.

XXIX

Bangladesh, Chittagong

The skeletons of the ships sat on the beach in the sun like the carcasses of stranded whales, Swirls of oil lay in the bilges of those which hadn't quite melted away. The odd seabird floated around in the water or glided by in the breeze, but the oil was the only other organic matter in the vicinity. The fish were all poisoned years earlier.

Some workers laboured in the bowels of one leviathan, salvaging everything which could be melted or crushed and sold. They took puffs on their shared cigarettes while they tugged away at the asbestos lagging which they had to remove to get at some pipework. The fibres fluttered around them. They were oblivious to the harmful qualities of the environment in which they worked, which was lucky for them as they had no alternative source of employment anyway.

One of them took too long a puff and then saw the owner of this breakers glaring at him from a railing high up in the gutted engine room. He passed the cigarette over and mumbled something and his companion flicked a gaze at the owner and then took one quick drag and cast the butt aside.

The owner lingered for a while. His was a competitive business. He had no room for malingerers. Workshy employees who didn't turn up, but cried off sick weren't paid. His operation was not a charity. He had his son at his side, who was dressed very smartly and wore glasses to compensate for the eye problems that his enforced studies were causing him. "You see," said his father, pointing to the workers. "People will try to cheat you. You must be strong."

"But you say you want me to be a politician, father, not a businessman like you." The boy was speaking English, not Bangla. His father insisted on that.

"True, but even politicians have employees. In fact, if you make it to the top, the whole Bangladeshi population will comprise of your employees. I should go down there and strike them, but I am too old for those steep steps. "Come. It is not healthy here. I just like to appear on the odd Saturday to make sure there is no more than the minimum slacking."

"Yes, father,"

They climbed down the ladders built into the scaffolding and looked around them. "Father, do you think one day there will be no more ships?"

"That's a strange question," said the man. "No one can dismantle these vessels more cheaply and profitably than us," he replied. He looked along the beach to the next spot, which had a freshly-beached vessel on the sand. "Ah, I am too soft, that is my problem. I have a generous heart. I do not squeeze everyone enough. Look at my business rivals. They are all millionaires while I struggle along making a pittance. I can barely afford your school fees, but I never hesitate to make sacrifices for my family."

"Thank you, father."

"Come along, son." The man looked at a small boy trotting up with his father's lunch. He recognised him. His father was one of the two workers stripping out the asbestos lagging. The boy, who was about the same age as his own son, paused at their side and looked up at him. The man toyed with the idea of giving him a coin and then, sensibly, in his mind, restrained himself and substituted a pat on the head. He didn't want word to get around that he was a soft touch. Confused, the boy began rushing up the scaffold like a squirrel.

"Father," said his son, "why is he poor and I am not?"

"You want to be poor?"

"No, I just wondered..."

"Concentrate on your schoolwork and one day you might be in a position to help the poor."

"Like you, father?" The man frowned.

"You ask too many questions."

"But how am I going to learn?"

"The poor are poor and the not poor are not poor; that is life," said the man. He continued on his way over the sand to his waiting Mercedes, his confused son trailing him.

XXX

Bangkok

"Yeah?" said Garnet into his mobile. He was trying to cross the junction at Nana Plaza which was a death-defying action. The little green man was lit but this was just an indication that if you were thinking of trying to cross the road, this was probably a good time for it.

"Garnet?" said a strange voice, which had the odd quality of seeming a touch effeminate, but tough at the same time.

"Yeah, this is Garnet.

"This is Big Gay Bob?"

"Are you kidding?"

"Something funny?" Now the voice just sounded tough.

"Not at all," Garnet replied. "Do go on."

"I found out you want to know where this Russian guy is."

"Oh yeah?"

"Yeah, I run a beach bar." The American mentioned the name of an island. "That British kid on the other touristy island here, mentioned this to me."

"Yeah, I was going to come down for another look."

"Don't bother, I can tell you where this Russian is, pal."

"And?" The American gave him the name of a

nearby town on the mainland, and some directions within the town. "Why do you want to give me this information?" Asked Garnet.

"Do you care?"

"Just interested."

"I don't like violence. This kid beat up some British guy. I had enough violence in Nam. And I came here for a quiet life."

"And?"

"I hate commies."

"And?"

"And I hate Russians, generally."

"He still with that girl?"

"Yeah."

"Where did you get your information? I just want to know the source so I can judge its reliability."

"The local fishermen."

"O.K. Well, thanks, Gay Bob."

"It's either Big Gay Bob or just Bob."

"Thanks, Big Gay Bob."

"You're more than welcome. pal." The American hung up.

Garnet stood staring at his mobile while being buffeted by sex tourists and kids riding scooters along the pavement. That was easy, he thought.

XXXI

Bangkok

Roman sat on the Aeroflot flight in business class, waiting impatiently while it taxied up to the stand at Suvarnabhumi. He looked every inch what he was, an ex-KGB colonel, now a member of the "kinder, gentler" KGB, the SVR. His bald egg-shaped head, which normally glistened with sweat as soon as temperatures rose about fifteen degrees, and his steel-rimmed eyeglasses and his aggressive stance gave the game away. All the requests for foreign postings had just been laughed at earlier during his career. One boss, who'd worked out of the Los Angeles consulate, had told him, "The Americans and British have a phrase, 'straight out of central casting'. Sometimes, we can soften the edges, but with you even trying would just be a waste of time." But now Roman had enough authority to send himself on trips.

The door opened and some of the humid air managed to squeeze through the gap between the plastic of the airbridge and the hull of the aircraft. Instantly, Roman's pate was glistening. The cute brunette stewardess who'd served in business class smiled at him. Ramon ignored her. Roman had never very been interested in women and certainly not in airline stewardesses. The stewardess's grin remained. This early morning flight from Sheremetyevo was known as the mobster special. Friendly smiles from the passengers were not often in evidence.

Roman carried nothing more than an attaché case and a small cabin bag. He wouldn't be staying long. His diplomatic passport saw him through control very quickly and then he was looking around the arrivals hall. Alexander approached him. Roman looked with distaste at the other man's clothing: a pair of slacks and the sort of cheap jacket married men wore. Roman, himself, was in a hand-tailored suit.

They went to the lifts which led to the carpark. "You didn't come with a driver. He could have waited at the kerb."

"You said low-profile and they don't allow it anyway," said Alexander. He stared at the lift buttons. "I could have handled this, you know."

"How did you come to have such a stupid brother?"

"Different father. My father was KGB; his was a street sweeper. My mother married him after my father was sent to the gulags.”

“That’s what happens when you indulge in conspiracies.”

“He was innocent.”

“Careful, Alexander. In Russia, no one is innocent.” Alexander would have sulked if he didn’t have ice in his veins. He thought of their coming mission.

“I could have handled this myself,” he repeated.

“You had your chances.”

“I believed him.”

“Then you’re a fool.” Alexander knew that it would take years for his career to recover from this and if he didn’t get things under very firm control, very quickly, he wouldn’t even have to worry about his career; it would be over. “How is your wife?”

“Well, thank you, Roman.”

“She was the best secretary I ever had.” And the prettiest, thought Alexander, not that you would be any more interested in that kind of thing than I am. The door opened and they went out to the car.

“You will stay at your usual hotel.”

“Of course.”

“When do you want to go down?”

“Tomorrow.”

“You didn’t give me much notice, you know.”

“Your stupid brother,” said Roman, shaking his head. “Incredible.” Alexander jiggled the flaps and switches and the German leviathan edged its way through the parked cars, trailing an elderly Thai woman in a Honda. “This is too conspicuous. I don’t want you driving it anymore.”

“My wife insists...”

“Do I employ you or your wife.”

“You employ me.

“Good.” Alexander wondered if American spy chiefs spoke to their operatives like this.

XXXII

Southern Thailand

Petrov frolicked in the sand with Ludmilla. He took a look around him at the bushes and saw only a couple of little boys, poking at something with a stick, and whipped her panties off. "Petrov," she squeaked as he made love to her." She looked to her side as she squirmed, and saw the boys. They hadn't appeared to notice anything unusual. "They might get their parents."

"This is not Abu Dhabi." Petrov finished too quickly and rolled off her and propped himself up on his elbows, looking out at the sea.

"You shouldn't have beaten that boy up," said the girl, idly, poking at the sand with her index finger.

"I've been beating up other boys over you for years. You enjoy it. Gives you a thrill." She sat up and clutched at his arm.

"Petrov," she said. "Don't say that." She relaxed and lay back in the sand. "Why did you leave me?"

"I told you why. I thought you would be safer alone."

"But then..."

"I couldn't stand the thought of life without you."

"Where can we run?"

"Brazil."

"Petrov, you are crazy."

"I'm not."

"How can we even get there?"

"Through the U.S."

"Petrov that's impossible."

"I'm working on it and when we get there, I have a contact, an uncle of a friend from the Navy who jumped ship from a reefer boat, thirty years ago."

"You should have just..."

“Don’t.”

“He’s your own brother.”

“Half-brother.” He turned to look down at her tanned face and swept her hair from her forehead. “Listen. There is no Alexander. He’s a computer program, a hologram. You can’t work for the SVR if you have any soul. They tell you to shoot some woman or old man or child, you shoot him. That’s it. Nothing to discuss. And I wouldn’t be off the hook with the Government, only with him.”

“You shouldn’t drink. You shouldn’t. When you drink, you have a big mouth.” Petrov looked at the sand and flexed his massive biceps, the hula girls who were tattooed on them doing a little dance as he did.

“They left them down there to die,” he said. “Imagine that, four days trapped in a hull, believing that people were coming, and no one was coming.”

“Putin is the top man. Sometimes top men have to take tough decisions.”

“I had friends on that boat and they had families.”

“The families were looked after.” Petrov scoffed. “They were. It said so on the television.” She pulled her bikini pants up; she hadn’t been wearing a top. “Don’t want to get my lady bits sunburnt.”

“Uggg.”

“Oh Petrov, you are so old-fashioned. You would have been better off in Soviet days.”

“My father thought the Soviet Government was wonderful, do you know that? What did they ever do for him? Made him sweep streets all day just so he could afford to buy cigarettes. Just brain-washing.”

“Hah. You don’t like the new Government, you don’t like the old Government. You don’t want any government.”

“There’s not much government in Brazil.”

“How will we get though the U.S.A.?”

“I’m working on it.”

“The weather is always hot in Brazil.”

"Yes, no more freezing Russian winters for you." Petrov rolled over onto his front and saw a policeman standing next to the little boys. "Unbelievable," he said. "The little bastards went and got the cops. He won't do anything, though. I don't think he saw anything. I don't care anyway."

"Shall we go back into town?"

"We ought to. I am expecting something, anyway."

"What are you expecting?"

"Something someone's been working on." He looked at her pulling her flip flops on. "You won't shut up until I tell you, will you?"

"You wouldn't want me to change, would you?"

"You're soon going to be a U.S. citizen."

XXXIII

Bangkok

The Thai assassin's translator listened to Smirnov. "Poison?" he queried.

"One of those fish poisons. You understand?" The translator was offended, but didn't let it show in his voice.

"We understand, but he can't get down there that quickly. Smirnov bit his lip. Normally, he had perfect control over his emotions, but he was under a lot of strain.

"Then farm it out?"

"What?"

"Give it someone else, someone trustworthy."

"Yes, but then the fee will be bigger. We have to pay him and my client needs his commission."

"O.K., ten per-cent more."

"Twenty,"

"Do not bargain with me."

"You have someone else who can do this for

you?" Alexander's blood was boiling.

"Fine, but I'll remember this."

"Is that a threat." Alexander's grip on his mobile tightened. "You think we fear you?" Alexander bit his lip.

"Just get it done. Be professional."

"We don't fail." Alexander went back inside the hotel room, having slipped out onto the balcony to make his call. He found Roman's merciless eyes were boring into him. He'd thought the man'd be a while longer in the bathroom.

"To whom were you speaking?"

"Some relative in the States."

"You seemed very stressed."

"They don't listen, you know. They get to America and then they don't listen." I took too long to make a decision; I lingered, thought Alexander. I shouldn't have lingered. Families. You're at their mercy.

XXXIV

Southern Thailand

The fisherman in the southern town got the call. "Difficult," he said.

The Bangkok-based assassin was silent for a while. Once the silence had lingered long enough, he said, "Do you want the job or not?"

"I didn't say I didn't want it," said the Southerner.

"There is no time to waste. Go and do it now. And tip off the doctor so that there are no problems later on. He will sort out the coroner. I want them unconscious and, officially, slowly dying." The Bangkok man thought. "Or rapidly dying. But they can't be speaking to anyone. And the boy can't be recovering. I want the girl to recover eventually, but not soon.

"They'll be in a coma."

"Good."

"How are the hospitals in that town?"

"There is one good one and one not so good."

"See they get taken to the not-so-good one."

"O.K. It's a shame we can't do a rape and murder."

"Don't deviate."

"I was just saying."

"This is for Russians. You know what they're like. They don't like deviations."

"O.K. Is the girl beautiful?"

"What's that got to do with anything?"

"It'd just be a shame, that's all."

"Do I have to give this to someone else?"

"No." The fisherman was thinking of the new Jeep he would buy, an American one. They were junk, but they were status symbols.

"And don't spend the money for a month."

"I'm a professional."

XXXV

Southern Thailand

The doctor listened to the machines beeping and looked with satisfaction at his two patients. The girl was good-looking. With a normal poisoning, they both might have had a chance of a rapid recovery, especially the boy; he looked very fit. "What a shame we have no idea where they ate," he said to his nurse."

"Have you notified the Thai authorities, too?"

"Of course. Don't you think I know how to do my job?" He had propositioned her a while ago and she had rejected him, a rejection which still caused rancour. He wondered when the other Russians would arrive. They were probably still arguing at the other hospital, the one to which they had been misdirected. The doctor actually liked Russians. They were generally open to the idea of paying to queue jump. Many times, he'd plucked a just-arrived, bleeding bar fighter out of the waiting room ahead of women and children who'd been waiting for hours.

"Do you think they'll survive?"

"Ah, well, we have to find out what they're suffering from first etc. etc."

"Why are the Russian consulate people coming so quickly? Even the British consulate normally takes longer."

"The Russians probably care more for their citizens," said the doctor. He was aware of a sinister presence behind him and turned to see Roman and Smirnov. The bald-headed one looked at him. "Poisoning," said the doctor, with a shrug. "Happens all the time with youngsters. They like to think they're being experimental and living the true Thai experience."

"You know what it is?"

"We have only an idea. It will be some kind of fish."

"Convenient."

"I beg your pardon." The doctor looked from one to the other. He could detect anger and frustration in the bald-headed one, but the younger Russian looked to be completely without emotion. "Have you notified their families?"

"I am his family," said the younger one. Smirnov moved over to his brother's bedside. "He always was a stupid boy."

"You are so sure he's going to die?" said Roman suspiciously. Smirnov said nothing.

"Our sympathies," said the doctor.

"Do you think there is any chance?" said Roman. The doctor shrugged. Not with the boy, seeing as I haven't even given him sufficient antidote, he thought.

"There is always some hope. But, until I get the lab report, I don't know what they ate or how much. It's not good."

"You don't seem too surprised, Alexander," said Roman. The nurse looked confused but the doctor poked her and her polite, uninterested expression reappeared.

"I am in shock."

"You have too much training for that, Alexander." They walked out of the room.

"It's what we wanted, anyway," said Alexander, quietly.

"You know we like to send a message."

"You can still put a bullet in his brain."

"Don't be petulant, Alexander. Anyway, in the hospital?" Alexander couldn't wait to have a secret cigarette once the senior man was gone. "It still seems to me to be quite a coincidence."

"Petrov always was stupid."

"I hope you have not been stupid, too, Alexander."

Once they were at the airport, Roman went off alone to the toilets and rang his staff. "Get me Smirnov's mobile records for yesterday," he said.

XXXVI

Bangkok

The Kiwi and the French lady sat in the back of the Kiwi's nineteen-seventies Bentley. Shane looked on, facial tattoos shifting as he squinted in the sunlight which poured through the front passenger windows and changed his expression from one of scorn to one of confusion.

"You two are perhaps encroaching on my business?" said the French lady. Her Eurasian features and diminutive form kept bringing to mind in both the Kiwi and Shane the impression that she was one of their employees and they had to constantly fight to remind themselves that she was Bangkok's premier vice queen. The Kiwi stretched, his head rising another few inches, and turned to face her and looked down his beaky nose. The steel-rimmed spectacles which he wore gave him the air of a senior cancer specialist studying a radiograph.

"My dear Elodie," he began. The French Lady's face flushed.

"Don't use my name," she said. "Only my father is permitted to call me that." The Kiwi smiled. He'd deliberately incited this burst of rage in order to put her on the defensive.

"Madame," he said, inclining his head with a mock gesture of obeisance. "We are quite happy with our current enterprises. We do not wish to go head to head with you. You deal in reality; we deal with fantasy. On occasion, our girls will indulge the odd British public-school boy with his mild S and M fantasy scenarios, but we do not like severity. You are a sadist; we, on the other hand, are simply businessmen. Shane?" Shane chipped in.

"It's not worth it. We're worth millions, already." The Kiwi frowned. He was worth the millions; Shane was an employee.

"Someone is."

"Whom?" said Shane. He said 'whom' because he thought that this was the posh version of who and he was trying to appear sophisticated. The Kiwi hid his irritation.

"I thought you were."

"And he's operating out of where?"

"Why do you assume it's a man?" The Kiwi sighed. Even vice queens were getting on board with this feminist thing now.

"And he or she is operating out of where?" You do realise the pronoun 'he' is non-gender specific in such a sentence construction." Shane's brow creased.

"The TBAS," suggested the French Lady.

"Hmmm. That's mainly Brits. They don't do much business like that in Bangkok. They're happy with their bars and... Well, just bars. They're too lazy to get on. As soon as they're making enough to support their Thai wife's relatives, they lose their motivation."

"Of course. So, who is behind him?"

"The Persian?"

"Not his scene. He's only interested in smoking his shisha pipe and reclining on cushions with his paid girlfriends."

"So, you'll want to be careful, then. Don't dive in until you know."

"It's not just domination."

"Dressing up? Who cares?"

"Don't be stupid." The Kiwi bristled. "I mean, you know…," the French Lady continued, worried that she had gone too far.

"No, I don't know."

"Snuff." The Kiwi was brought up short.

"You've got to stop that. We had all this out ten years ago. It just brings too much heat down on all of us."

"Aren't you listening? I'm not the one doing it."

"Shane?"

"Honestly, boss. I haven't heard anything."

"Clients? Please tell me Asians, so it's nothing to do with us."

"Anglo's. Farangs."

"Great. So, our problem, too. Why don't you just pick up whomever is the middle man and do your thing. The unlovely Chang can get the information out of him quite speedily, I'm sure."

"Not until I know who's behind him. Like you said, I don't want to dive in."

"This is a drag," said Shane.

"Don't give me your comic-book dialogue," hissed the French lady. "You just find out what you can and I'll find out what I can."

"Incidentally," said the Kiwi, "how much is the going rate?"

"You're not serious?"

"Just interested from a business point of view. I told you, it's too much hassle for us and we're a kindlier, gentler kind of vice organisation, more Las Vegas."

"But topless and sometimes bottomless," said Shane.

"Las Vegas is topless, you moron," said the French Lady. "Stop this heap of junk; I want to get out. Who drives British cars? German engineering is the best. I'm embarrassed you picked me up in this." At a signal from the Kiwi, the driver pulled over to the kerb and the French Lady opened her door.

"Goodbye," said the Kiwi, too quietly for her to hear above the sound of the traffic.

"What do you think?" said Shane, once the French Lady had tried to slam the door and been defeated by the luxury vehicle's mechanisms.

"Her problem. She's just offended, that's all."

"I thought she cared for the plight of these young ladies." The Kiwi tried to smile.

XXXVII

Bangkok

Garnet was stunned. He sat in his office, gently pushing his swivel chair to and fro and chewed the end of a fake Biro, one of a box of fifty which Petunia had bought in a bid to cut down on costs in the long term and only about three of which worked. He flung the expatriates' newspaper onto the desk.

"And?" said Petunia, smiling sweetly.

"The Russians died."

"The boy."

"Yep, and his girlfriend."

"The girl who went missing and then turned out only to have been keeping quiet on another island."

"Her." He flung the pen down on top of the paper. "Why did you buy these? They don't even work?"

"You just use them as chew toys, anyway." Garnet dialled a number on his mobile while a little voice in his head was telling him 'don't ring; don't ring'. "I want to talk to you," he said, once someone had answered.

"The usual place," said the voice at the other end of the line.

Garnet hovered on a platform of anxiety, sucking on Thai cigarettes in a vain attempt to reduce his gnawing sense of worry. Two girls passed the end of the alleyway which was behind his office and one giggled, causing him to look up. Just as he did, the third secretary from the British Embassy came round the corner, his eyes fixated on Garnet's scruffy figure.

"Garnet," he said, "you look more American every day. Flower shirts for Americans; England football shirts for Brits, especially the red ones. You know that." He seemed to be thinking. "Is that the away kit?" he added idly. "I don't follow football."

"What did you get me into?" asked Garnet. The third secretary just looked at him. "I don't want this MI6 'don't worry about it' line."

"What are you going on about? You want work. Business is not good. The internet's finally getting through to loveless British pensioners and they're not taking the emotional risks they were. You were paid, weren't you?"

"You read that they died." The third secretary sighed with annoyance.

"Fish poisoning, Garnet. Happens all the time to the young and stupid."

"It said they haven't even got the results back yet."

"It's always fish poisoning, Garnet. Anyway, even if it weren't, why the sudden attack of anxiety? Do you really care?"

"You're supposed to be enemies, you and Smirnov."

"Garnet, there are no enemies in the intelligence community. It's one big pantomime.

Anyway, do you really think Smirnov would arrange the assassination of his own brother?"

"He's Russian."

"They're bigger on families than the Jews, Garnet. You know your problem: you ask too many questions. Once a policeman, always a policeman. He couldn't have his own people looking for a member of his family. That's all there was too it. Someone was missing. You found him. He was young and stupid. He ate raw fish without even knowing what it was; he died. It's just another case of idiot youngsters travelling to unknown parts, and then suffering through their own naivete, like those Western teenage girls who go home with 'chicken fried noodles' in Thai script tattooed on their arms instead of 'love is life' or whatever."

"You're setting me up to get kicked out."

"I wouldn't involve foreigners in something like that, would I? Anyway, I've given up trying to get you kicked out. The Home and Foreign offices like you being here; the Thais' Special Victims Unit like you being here, well they like dealing with Petunia but they know she'd accomplish nothing on her own; and, more importantly, our ambassador seems to like you."

"And the Americans."

"The Americans will turn on you one day, Garnet. Americans don't have friends. It's all about business. The Godfather didn't portray the Mafia, it portrayed America. Why are you suddenly conscience stricken?"

"He ran away. He deserted that girl. Then he came back, beat up some British moron and tried to disappear again, this time with his girl."

"The plot thickens!" said the third secretary, derisively. Do yourself a favour and shut up. You know your problem, Garnet: you never learn. Seriously, smarten yourself up. Where's that Sammy the Sikh suit with the zombies lining?" He smiled. "Come on. Cheer up. You're in the clear."

"Just tell me what happened."

"I already told you. Now you're beginning to irritate me, and you'll begin to irritate the Russians. Once you start to irritate foreigners, or, at least those on our own side, like the Russians, you will be on the path to upsetting our own government and then you're out, back to whatever South London hovel you appeared from, except you won't be able to afford to live there anymore because your hovel will have some media luvvie living in it who won't sell it for under a million."

"Since when were Russians on the same side?"

"Since China threatened the Post War order, Garnet. They're the new Soviet Union. We had hot wars, then the cold war and now something more sinister. I can see the wheels turning. No, this is nothing to do with China. If it were, I wouldn't mind how much you stirred it up. Listen to your Petunia."

"You know something," said Garnet, "I've always thought you fancied her."

"Don't do ladyboys, Garnet, not even post-operative ones. This is a warning, a serious one. You irritate me. I don't like you. I don't like having you around but you can consider that this warning as not being from me. You did your job; you were paid. it's over. I don't want to talk about this again. Got it?" There was a pause while Garnet ground his cigarette butt into the dirt in the cracks in the concrete. "I didn't hear you Garnet."

"All right."

"What?"

"Got it."

"Good. Don't call again. We call you sometimes; you don't call us. Remember?" Garnet wondered if the man would wait there until he had an affirmation, but the third secretary just grinned, his face becoming even uglier with the combination of the yellow incisors and the beaky nose so like the Kiwi's displayed, and then turned and went back out onto the main street.

Garnet's tension dissipated with his

disappearance. I tried, he said to himself.

XXXVIII

Bangkok

Garnet faced Petunia and then looked at the photocopied passport details page in his hand and sighed. "So, it was him." Petunia looked guilty.

"You Thais are communal. Something like this happens in Thailand and you all feel ashamed. Still, I'm glad they found him even if... Poor woman.

"You've never been married, Garnet. People get worried and they suffer from shame. They want to keep bringing in the..."

"The moolah. So, for whom was he working? He flew out to join a ship that had vanished.

"I don't see how you can hide a ship."

"There are seventy-eight thousand commercial ships in the world, Petunia. They change names and owners all the time. Authorities can be bribed; people can be threatened.

"There's more."

"What?" She didn't answer him and Garnet quickly grew impatient.

"What?" he demanded.

"They wanted to send photos of the bloated corpse."

"To whom?"

"To the wife. They hate open stories of foreigners disappearing. It's terrible publicity.

"Jesus."

"Don't Garnet. You..."

"You're not even... O.K. I'm..."

"Sorry?" said Petunia with a little smile. Garnet grinned. "Garnet, don't you think we can find some way to solve this?" Garnet was thinking.

"The chief engineer sent out to join a ship which had disappeared on which he worked years previously, identified as possibly having been killed by some possibly Russian dude in a dilapidated seamen's hotel and then found bloated and floating in a filthy canal. So, if the ship still exists, it's in Thailand. What did he put on his immigration card?"

"Just tourist."

"So, no way to trace which shipping agent picked him up, if any. Andre thought it went missing, rather than sank. Do some investigation, Petunia. Hang out around the shipyards. Go and talk to the tanker terminal staff. When you find some information bring me in. Until then, I'd best stay behind the scenes. Don't want to frighten any Thais. None will want to give information to a foreigner."

Outside Bangkok

Petunia had trailed around seamen's bars and bluffed her way into oil terminals to badger mooring men and flash the photographs of the vessel. "I don't know," one said. "Who cares? One tanker is the same as another. I was at sea, myself; all shipowners are crooks anyway. The only difference between any of them is that some are in jail and the rest should be. And this all sounds a little frightening if you don't mind my saying."

In one terminal, she had been thrown out of an office. In another she had been propositioned by some workers and then threatened with rape. Sometimes, she thought that Garnet didn't pay her enough.

How do you find a ship when nobody wants it found. Why couldn't they just say it had sunk and give it up. Because Andre's fee was too great and because a chief engineer had flown out to re-join a vessel which wasn't supposed to exist anymore.

She finally went to the surrounds of the shipyard which was likeliest to have had a vessel like this in it. They flatly refused to let her inside, her pleas attracting laughter, and she slumped into a worker's eatery opposite the shipyard gates. She was sitting on a stool at the counter, it being half an hour before the lunch period and a good time to talk to the owner when the owner walked over to her.

"You won't do any business in here," he said. "And certainly not dressed like that. An office-worker look. Never seen that before."

"Maybe I am a genuine office worker."

"Yeah, good one."

"I'm looking into something." She flipped a business card out of her purse onto the counter. The owner spun it across the Formica and read it.

"Hmm," he said. "A detective agency? Cargo stolen? Happens. I heard of an entire oil cargo being stolen once."

"They found them that time. They shipped the oil off and then scuttled the boat. "I'm looking into a missing ship, but it was empty when it went missing."

"Maybe it sank."

"It went into some Chinese port a while ago and never left..."

"How could..."

"The port denies it ever arrived. It's just a tiny port. The local authorities back up the port, and they wouldn't put any effort into a search and rescue effort, as if they knew it would be a waste of time."

"And..."

"There've been rumours that it's been in Thailand." The owner stepped back from the bar.

"It's funny you say that." he said. He indicated a young boy in a boiler suit sitting with some other workers. "Some welder," he said. "Actually, he's more than just some welder, he's my godson. Skiver. In here early every dinnertime. Went off to Singapore, but came running home to mummy, stupid boy. Anyway."

"Anyway?"

"He said there was something funny about a boat in the yard. This was just a while ago."

"A long while or a little while?"

"Little while. Very little."

"And."

"Something not right." Obviously, thought Petunia with frustration. Then the bell on the door started tinging and the place started to fill up. She managed to retain her seat at the bar despite being squeezed on all sides. The owner seemed to have forgotten about her, but eventually he caught her eye and nodded at the little group in boiler suits. "Go on," he said, "Speak to them." Just then, a farang walked in. There was some shifting in the crowd and a passage to the counter opened up. The farang happily used it to shove his way to the front. "I'm Moses parting the red sea, only it's a yellow sea," he said. Even the few Thais who understood English failed to laugh. Petunia glanced at him and then turned to face the counter, hoping that he wouldn't notice her in the long mirror. She needn't have worried. Face hidden, she just seemed, in her pinstripe jacket, to be some office worker who'd decided to slum it this lunchtime. She cast an eye in the mirror to see the welder slipping out and then climbed down off her stool, taking care to turn with her face away from the farang and went outside. The owner looked after her with surprise and then at the much too large sum which she'd left on the counter.

Petunia caught up with the welder further down the street. "Hey," she said. The man turned round.

"What?" he demanded, rudely.

"I just wanted to talk to you," she said.

"But what do you want? What do you want to talk about?" The man appeared to be looking over Petunia's shoulder in the direction from which she'd come. She saw fear on his face. Quickly, she darted a look behind her. The farang was standing outside the eatery, holding the door open with one hand, while he looked at them. The welder flushed and turned round and walked away as soon as Petunia whipped her head round.

Petunia wanted to turn round and look at the farang again, but just in case there was a chance he still hadn't recognised her, she thought it better to avoid him and carried on walking away. Once she'd reached a corner, she went round it and then sped up and turned some more corners and then paused for breath and dug her mobile out of her handbag.

"Garnet," she said, once the call had been answered.

"Yeah," said Garnet, in the laid-back tone which he normally only used after he'd just had sex with Jill. She could hear some squealing in the background, and high-pitched cackling, and her theory was confirmed. He was in the built-in hotel which was above the biggest ladyboy bar in Nana Plaza.

"That guy, the Australian."

"That narrows it down to about half a million people in Thailand."

"The horrible, obnoxious one everyone hates."

"O.K., down to about a quarter of a million; I still need you to be more specific."

"Goes into your Union Jack when he's in from Hong Kong. Garnet sat up, Jill flinging a long leg over him and sitting astride him

"Johnno?"

"Yes, him."

"And?"

"He's around this shipyard."

"Perhaps he's organising something for one of his yachts. Bit of overkill, mind, a full-scale shipyard, unless he's got one of those mobster's leviathans coming in. But they avoid commercial shipyards like the plague, even in emergencies."

"I was onto something."

"Oh yeah. I'm a little indisposed right now." Garnet tweaked one of Jill's nipples and she slapped him.

"Ow," he said. "That hurt. There's playing and there's domestic abuse."

"Garnet," said Petunia. She sounded

strained. "I think he might have recognised me. If there is something funny going on?"

"Get in a taxi."

"You want me to come to Nana Plaza. It'll take me an hour and a half." Garnet looked at Jill. He thought if Petunia did, he could send Jill back to Hanky Spankie's, see Petunia, and go upstairs and watch the spinning stage at Baccara. It was lingerie night, his favourite.

"Outside at the Reichstag," he said. He hung up and flipped over onto Jill.

The Reichstag as it was known by the Brits, or the Deutschland, as it was officially called, was very Bavarian, right down to the plump owner. Here the television could be tuned to show the Bundesliga or Grand Prix's on the occasions when Sebastian Vettel was likely to win, and, generally, there were no Brits making tired jokes about the war or nineteen sixty-six. The walls, did not, as they did at the Union Jack, feature warplanes of the host's nation, many Germans still being undecided as to whether they should be proud of their nation's Nazi past or ashamed of it. Michael Shumaker's portrait hung there, though, looking far more reminiscent of the Third Reich's ideal of the Master Race than a portrait of any run-of-the-mill Nazi officer would.

Garnet sat on a stool, ordered a beer from the Thai waitress dressed up like something out of the Sound of Music, a Thai beer, just to irritate Franz, the owner, and waited. Petunia came in, the doorbell clanging very loudly with typical German efficiency.

"Hey!" shouted Franz. "No transvestites."

"She's with me, Franz," said Garnet. "Transsexual, not transvestite you pock-marked oaf," he muttered. The pot-bellied German looked even more irritated than normal, but said no more, and Petunia slumped onto a stool at Garnet's table.

A welder," she said. "He knows something. His godfather runs the canteen opposite the shipyard."

"Which shipyard." Petunia told him. "And?"

"He might have talked, but this Johnno came in and he ran away."

"Who ran away, Johnno or the welder?"

"The welder."

"So, go back another time."

"He looked frightened.

"Frightened of Johnno. Johnno's a clown. Probably did his fair share of bar-fighting in his time. Most Australians did. At least before they went all latte cafes and Pilates sessions. So, how do we lean on Johnno? Special Victims? Not unless he kills a hooker. Johnno's spiteful, but last I heard, he wasn't involved in any sexual shenanigans. He's a thief; he isn't a pervert.

"Everything's relative. Isn't that a British saying?"

"I'll get to him. You've done your bit." He squeezed her cheek. "Brave girl."

"Garnet, don't touch me like I'm some little... I'm not Jill." Garnet flushed.

"I'm sorry, Petunia," he said. Petunia smiled, timidly.

"It's all right. You were carried away. Isn't that the expression?" Garnet waved his hand in the air.

"Franz," he said, "glass of white wine." He looked at Petunia. "Crisps?" Petunia said nothing." "Just the white wine," said Garnet, loudly. Petunia knew the offer of crisps was Garnet's true apology. Normally, he wouldn't even bother buying her a drink.

XXXIX

Bangkok

The third secretary flipped through the file in front of him. The Chinese surveillance target looked back at him from the photograph. Despite his countrymen's ability to hide their feelings, there was a certain sense of his own superiority which appeared in the man's expression. Belt and roads, thought the third secretary; and tanks and fighter jets and napalm and God knows what else.

The information within the file had been obtained at great personal risk by an MI6 informant who had since disappeared in China. This wasn't abnormal. Many of MI6's informants disappeared, but they weren't told that during their 'interview' of course. The service was fairly sure, however, that this had been over some other surveillance which the man had been doing, and was willing to take a chance that the victim had chomped down on his cyanide pill prior to Chinese state torture and hadn't blabbed about his other projects.

So, you like that sort of thing, do you, thought the third secretary while continuing to examine the photo. It's always the quiet ones. He'd sought approval from home, and received it, kind of, in the usual form, phrased so that the sender could claim misinterpretation if the operation ended in disaster.

Carefully, the third secretary laid the file down on his desk and pushed himself backwards and bit his lip and wondered. If this were successful, it could see him sent back home, to the riverside, where skills in political manoeuvring and back-stabbing, which he believed he'd soon learn, were the qualities which put you on the route to the top.

He pondered life. It was sad that any success needed a victim, but that was just it. In order that someone shall succeed someone should fail. He wondered how Garnet was getting on. He hated Garnet. Just the thought of him filled him with fury. What was he: an incompetent merchant navy officer, obviously, or he wouldn't have been fired and let's forget all that rubbish about redundancy and foreign seafarers; a failed detective in the Metropolitan police, stupid enough to cross the masons and refuse to give up on trying to jail some vicious East

End crime lord; and a bottom feeder private detective in Bangkok. And Petunia? Don't even go there as our American chums say. A post-operative transsexual. The third secretary understand how Garnet would need a local on the firm, but that! There was something frightening about post-operatives. Pre-operatives could be a joke. An incision, a bag of saline thrown into the medical waste bin and we were back to normal, but... The third secretary shuddered. His father, who had inherited the family money and blown it and had been lucky enough to attend a public school instead of a grotty comprehensive such as the one to which 'circumstances' had forced them to send him, would have said, 'ghastly'. Quite, thought the third secretary.

He turned his attention to the file again. How to lure him, that was the question. The third secretary had been an enthusiastic fly fisherman at home. This was similar: the deception, the luring. His office phone rang.

"Ambassador wants you," said the ambassador's secretary. The third secretary sighed. The ambassador's insistence on treating life as one big farce irritated him. So had his refusal to get rid of Garnet, but right now, he was grateful for that. He'd needed someone stupid and incompetent who would find what he wanted him to and no more, and Garnet had fit the bill.

"I'm coming right up," he said. He had no illusions that this would be about anything remotely worthwhile. It would concern some invitation and the question as to whether the invitees were likely to be suitable people with whom HRH's loyal ambassador to Bangers should be mingling.

XL

Southern Thailand

The doctor looked at the pile of large denomination Thai banknotes in his hand and listened to the criminals as they slammed the van doors and then had a quick discussion among themselves. Satisfied?" one said to him. He shrugged, then he thought he'd better display more enthusiasm.

"Most generous," he said. He listened to the insects in the shrubbery around the hospital's side door and lit up a cigarette.

"You shouldn't smoke," said one of the criminals. "You're a doctor you should know better."

"I suffer from stress," replied the doctor with a smile. "Aren't you going to leave someone in the back with her?"

"You think she'll die?"

"Of course not."

"Well then. We have a perfectly comfortable bench seat up front. No reason why one of use should perch on the wheel shrouding for eight hours," said one of them.

"Especially not when we think of your driving," said another, to the first speaker's annoyance.

"Hmm. Up to you. We could do this again," said the doctor. The leader of the criminals suddenly had a very angry expression upon his face.

"This never happened and won't happen again," he said. "This was a one off."

"Not even if I get some nice Western blonde."

"You're not listening,"

"O.K., O.K."

In the back of the van, Ludmilla lay, unconscious, but trussed up, just in case. She had a towel thrown across her stomach, but that was all. The leader of the criminals took a look through the little window. They all take time to shave their genitals, he thought. One of his relatives ran a backpackers and constantly had to clear out shower drains clogged with pubic hair. He turned round to the doctor again and the doctor misunderstood and thought the look of distaste on his face was caused by a reaction to himself. He threw his hands wide.

"I understand, O.K.?" he said, confusing the criminal.

"We're going now," said the man and then he and his companions climbed onto the van's seat and drove off through the manicured hospital grounds.

The doctor threw his cigarette onto the tarmac and ground it with his foot. Time to tell his wife about the new SUV. He would wake her up when he got home. Then he thought about things more carefully and decided to visit his mistress first. Fleeting thoughts of the pretty nurse who'd rejected him went through his mind, but she'd seemed a little suspicious when she'd turned up for duty and the Russian girl, who'd seemed to be getting better, had, apparently, died and been shipped off to the morgue so quickly. It wouldn't do to fling any cash at her in a further attempt at seduction, but the temptation was too great. The doctor didn't know it yet, though the morgue attendant would tell him in the morning, that the nurse had actually gone down there to have a look at the corpse and had been surprised to find it had already been shipped off to the crematorium.

The doctor turned round and went back into the hospital to change into that suit which the nice Sikh tailor in Bangkok had made for him. He whacked the wad of notes against the palm of his hand. Shame, he thought. If only I'd shown more talent, I could have been performing sex-change operations in Bangkok and making this kind of money day in, day out. Still, since the incident with the Phuket prostitute and the bungled tit job, he had to admit he'd been lucky to get any kind of medical position.

XLI

Shanghai

Garnet sat in Andre's offices in the tower beside the river in Shanghai. The view was magnificent. He couldn't help diverting his gaze from Andre's rotund, face, which, despite his new-found wealth, still bore the same black-rimmed spectacles which he'd worn at maritime college. "So, do you get the key to the executive bathroom?"

"I have my own bathroom," replied Andre, testily.

"Is it really a bathroom or just a toilet which you call a bathroom?"

"Nice to see you're still as irritating as ever. Some things never change, eh? That's comforting in a rapidly developing city like Shanghai. I don't know why you had to visit Shanghai. Could have gone straight to Yantau if you wanted to investigate on the spot."

"You know I came here in '91 on a log carrier. We brought them from Washington State. Longview. Criminal, really. Raping the environment like that. It's always the supposedly ethical, right-on states that do it, isn't it?"

"I believe Mississippi And Louisiana don't have any forests to rape," replied Andre. "You still have your tendency towards irrelevancy."

"The only Western business open was a single Kentucky Fried Chicken."

"Can we get to the matter in hand, please."

"So, no invitation to your home. Not quite the right sort of person, am I? Don't know which glass to use with which wine. I can't even tell red from white, you know. Can anyone? I've often wondered. Is it all just..."

"Garnet!"

"All right, I'm going. So, you can't tell me anything?"

"Not any more than I already told you on the

phone."

"Tell me about the owner." Andre tutted.

"Nigerian company."

"So, you don't know anything about him." Andre frowned. "You'll insure anything, won't you? You don't care if it goes down."

"It didn't go down. It's a small tanker. Tankers don't sink. Bulk carriers sink."

"Any sort of five-minute classification…"

"It's economics, Garnet. Not something I would expect you to know anything about. The world needs oil and iron ore to get into China and cheap Chinese junk to get out of China, or people starve. That's business."

"Will I be safe in Yantau?"

"Yeah. They killed an MI6 guy here a while ago and the British papers got to hear of it. The Chinese Government went mental. Caused so much stress. Don't think anyone's going to want to bump off a British guy for a while. You're not MI6, but even so. Ex-Metropolitan Police. That'd be bound to get some investigative journalist interested if you went missing."

"I thought President Xi threw them all out."

"Ha, it's like trying to…"

"Eat soup with a fork."

"Perfect description."

"I think it's a simile or maybe a metaphor. I still get those mixed up. Or maybe it's neither."

"Garnet, do me a favour and get out." Garnet stood up and grabbed a bundle of the cigars which Andre kept in a humidor on his desk for his flashier Chinese clients.

"I'll take some of these as an advance on my fee." He went over to the ludicrous, intricately carved, wooden door, which didn't go at all with the steel and glass which constituted the rest of the building. "So, it's a definite no on the invitation to the family pile, is it? Quite fancied your first wife, you know, the Brazilian?"

"Yes, I remember my first wife."

"You might have handed her over to me when you dumped her."

"Get out and do the job you're being paid to do." Garnet smiled and went out, leaving the door open. Andre's very sexy secretary, who was dressed in a very severe outfit, smiled at him, sweetly.

"You banging her, too?" shouted Garnet, over his shoulder.

XLII

Bangkok

The third secretary drifted through the TBAS while he tried to tune out the litany of complaints being voiced by the outraged-looking speaker. "My kids won't speak to me," the guy was saying, wiping away a tear. The audience was red-faced, joining him in his fury. They were indignant, their anger brought on by his litany of unfair judicial decisions. Maybe if you lost about ten stone, shaved, got a haircut and bought some decent clothes then your kids might want to know you, thought the third secretary. Having no interest in women, himself, he'd been spared the standard modern man's rite of passage of divorce, poverty, emotional turmoil and homelessness; and being not a very nice person, he didn't have much sympathy for those who hadn't.

He saw his quarry, a very shifty looking individual, slouched in a corner, drinking beer out of a plastic cup which the organisation bought with its subs as, once people's tempers had flared, there was a tendency for drinking vessels to be thrown around, especially by the Americans, who always seemed somehow to think that having a temper had to be evidenced by tantrum-like violence. The man caught sight of the third secretary moving towards him and shifted uncomfortably, looking for a path to an exit. There was none available; the crowd was too tightly packed.

"So," said the third secretary.

"So," repeated the man.

"We had a deal."

"Eh, yeah."

"And?"

"It's a lot more money. I paid up front. I bought her fair and square."

"Yeah, but we had a deal. I put you onto the seller."

"So, business is business."

"You know with whom you're dealing."

"With whom," repeated the man, with a sneer. "There's no way H.M. Government would approve something like this."

"Oh yeah. Princess Diana thought on similar lines. Didn't do her any good did it?" The man's face reddened. "The state can do anything it likes."

"I've got a deal with an American. He's willing to pay fifty."

"So, tell the Chinaman you want fifty. No skin of my nose. These people are addicts. They're like..."

"Yeah, but what if I don't want to upset my American client?"

"Listen, do you want to go on living? That's the question. Think about it." The man's jaw was jutting and his teeth were barred in a show of defiance, but the third secretary could tell he'd won. "If what I want to happen, doesn't happen, I'll have you turned over to the law. They'll be no mention of anything to do with the British Government at any trial. The judge won't allow it. You'll either do your time in a Thai prison and the guards will be made aware you started off with Thai girls, or you'll do it in a U.K. prison, which won't be that nice one in Portland with the Koi Carp that Gary Glitter's in that the Daily Mail is always on about; and sometime, you'll never know when it's going to happen, the connecting door to the section with the violent criminal element will be left open. Got it?" The man sulked. "Are you listening?"

"Persistent, aren't you?"

"You didn't answer."

"Got it."

"Good." The third secretary looked around him. "I don't know what the attraction is. You all come to this sexual Disneyland and then start to have meetings in which you moan about how terribly you were treated at home. It's like Jews escaping the holocaust and going to Palestine and then holding meetings where they all wind each other up about how terrible Auschwitz was."

"Jesus, you are really evil, to think up some comparison like that," said the man. The third secretary gave him a withering look. Then he drifted off into the crowd. He saw the man going up to a silver-haired, prosperous-looking guy whom he assumed was the soon-to-be disappointed client. The client smiled at him and put his arm around him and then stood away and glared at him, appearing to be infuriated. Good, thought the third secretary. Job done. Someone blew smoke in his face. He shot him a glance and resisted the impulse to punch him in the mouth, which would entail a lot of unwanted attention. Then he slipped out.

XLIII

Yantau, China, The Yellow Sea

Garnet got off the plane in Yantau and took a taxi into the city, telling the driver to take him to the top hotel. "This nothing," said the driver.

"Excuse me?" said Garnet leaning forwards.

"This nothing," said the driver, waving his hand to indicate the surrounding urban jungle. "Only rice."

"What?" The driver showed signs of frustration.

"Few years ago, only rice, now city." Ah, thought Garnet.

"Isn't that so for your whole country?" He didn't know if the driver understood him or not, but the man passed him a packet of Chinese cigarettes and suggested he took one, so he couldn't have been offended. They took a drive along the beach road and pulled up at the Pink Chrysanthemum; at least that's what the driver told him the huge Chinese characters on the side of the hotel said. Andre's company would pay the expenses, so Garnet saw no reason to stay in the sort of dosshouse to which he was accustomed.

A bellboy swept his trolly bag out of his hands and led the way to the desk and then deserted him. The Chinese girls smiled at him, photocopied his passport, handed it back to him with a room key and a leaflet for the massage centre on the sixth floor and smiled at him again. He looked around and then one of the girls pointed to the lifts.

As soon as he'd opened his room's door and found the bellboy opening his sliding doors to the balcony, tipped him, and thrown his Harris Tweed sports jacket, bought on a trip to London just so he'd always have something which reminded him of home, onto the bed, he'd taken the lift to the sixth floor and stripped off and slid onto the massage table. "You come from America?" asked the petite masseuse.

"I'm British," he replied. "but I live in Thailand." He relaxed, expecting a professional massage, but, after five minutes, the girl tapped him on the shoulder and then, once he'd strained his neck muscles to look up at her, she pushed her finger in and out of her mouth.

"You like?" she asked him.

"You're kidding," he said. "this is supposed to be a five-star hotel." She looked disappointed. "O.K.," he said, "but don't put it on the bill; I'll pay cash. O.K.?" He slumped down again. "I can force myself on occasion," he said.

In the evening, he made his way to the only venue in this city of half a million people in which you would be likely to find Westerners during their time outside work or home: a snooker hall. He slid up to the bar and bought himself a rum and coke and looked around him. A bearded white man was playing pool with another white man who was bald and seemed to be very cheerful. The bald man went round the table to pot an easy red and then looked up and saw him. He handed his pool cue to a bespectacled Chinese girl in tight jeans, slapped her ass, and came over to him. "You made it," he said. "What did you think of Shanghai?"

"Preferred it when it was communist," said Garnet. "Then it was the real China." The bald man looked confused.

"You couldn't get a shag in the old says," he replied. "And, anyway, look at you, you live and work in Soi Cowboy."

"I don't live and work in Soi Cowboy, Bodger. That's for Americans. I live and work in Nana."

"That's for Russians and Pakistanis."

"And poor Brits. The prices are low. The poor ones are the ones who get themselves into trouble. Who's the sweetie?"

"My fiancée." Garnet laughed. "I'm serious," said the other man.

"She must be twenty."

"Twenty-one."

"And you're fifty-five."

"As near as makes no difference."

"You've been here too long, Roger."

"Five years trying to build a three-hundred-foot gentleman's motor yacht with a gang of rice farmers." Roger smiled. He looked back at the table. "Ha," he said. "Florence just wiped out Malcolm." He looked at Garnet. "He's going to be the captain. Scottish."

"Good luck to him," said Garnet. "Did you ask around?"

"Aren't we going to talk about old times? You know? The Red Duster. The Empire on which the sun never set?"

"Pitcairn Island was just about the only colonial territory left by the time we went to sea, Roger." Roger straightened up and looked a little offended. Then he smiled. "Come and meet Malcolm."

"I don't want to meet any miserable Scottish git."

"He's all right. Only thing is, he doesn't whore around."

"So, what then? Airfix kits, that type of thing?"

"He's an intellectual. Reads books on consciousness. You know. Yeah, I don't understand it either, but each to his own."

Later on, Roger sat with a girl on his knee in the KTV while he belted out Goldfinger in a particularly tuneless voice. Once he'd finished, he turned to Garnet and said, "You need to try a trumpet."

"What's a trumpet?" asked Garnet, and Malcolm leant in to him and said, "You don't want to know."

Once Roger had slid off into one of the private rooms, leaving the huge screen displaying the lyrics of Don't Cry for me Argentina, Malcolm suggested that they abandoned him. Garnet raised an eyebrow. "He's a big boy," said the Scotsman.

Outside, listening to the cicadas in the manicured bushes, Garnet looked around him.

"You know," he said, "China can be O.K., sometimes."

"So, you want to know about the missing tanker."

"Roger told you."

"He did. Listen, turn up at the yard in the morning."

XLIV

The shipyard, Yantau: China, The Yellow Sea

Garnet climbed out of the taxi and trudged through the mud to the dilapidated portakabins, glancing at the enormous, antiquated-looking motor yacht which sat alongside the wharf, gently bobbing in the water as the odd tug passed it creating a mini swell. Once he was inside the little complex, he looked around him. A Chinese girl, cradling a filthy yard cat, looked at him and then rapped on a door at her side. "What!" said Roger from his office. He flung open the door. "Oh. Hi," he said.

"Malcolm invited me to have a look around," said Garnet.

"You abandoned me," said Roger, accusingly.

"You were in good hands." Roger's face broke into a smile.

"Malcolm's in there," he said, pointing to the door opposite.

Garnet went into the other office and saw Malcolm counting out piles of Renminbi while a pretty young blonde with a ponytail simpered, and pleaded with him to permit her to remain in an apartment instead of moving onto the yacht. Malcom looked up and nodded at Garnet, but continued with the conversation with the girl.

"So," he said, "just because you're having sex with one of the Scandinavians you think you're entitled to continue living in an apartment for which, incidentally, you still expect the owner to pay." Some other white man at another desk winced. The girl pouted, grasped the clipboard she had been holding in her hand, close to her chest and went over to the door.

"Excuse me," she said, indignantly, to Garnet, who was blocking her path. Garnet nimbly stepped aside and took a good look at her arse as she went, in an attempt at revenge for his humiliation.

Malcom threw down the last wad of rubber-banded cash, scooped it all up, thrust it into a safe, locked it, pocketed the key and said, "Follow me." Garnet followed him along the quay. "What do you think of the boat?" said the Scotsman.

"What is it, a copy of the S.S. Great Britain or something?"

"Not far off." A thin youth, holding what appeared to be a bag of vomit, followed them into a little rubber boat and fired up the outboard.

"Why's that kid carrying a bag of vomit around?" asked Garnet.

"That's his lunch," said Malcolm, without a smile.

They motored across the port and tied up to a fishing boat and the kid shouted up at the gunwale and a toothless old man appeared. "This kid is a gofer for us," said Malcolm. "Sleeps in the yard, would you believe? This is some relative of his. This boy is plugged-in, believe it or not. He knows more about what is going on around here than the officials. I went to him when Roger blurted out that you were on your way, just fishing for information. You brought cash with you, didn't you?"

"Of course."

"Time to start paying it out. Don't even think of stiffing them." They tied the boat up and went on board the fishing boat. A scholarly-looking, rail-thin kid appeared. "This is Rick, my translator," said Malcolm.

"I am delighted to make your acquaintance," said Rick. Then the fishing boat skipper started talking. "They found a corpse, with his hands tied behind his back, floating outside. The corpse did not look Chinese."

"Filipino?"

"Yes," There was some more Mandarin.

"On the night on which the tanker came in for fuel, there were foreigners around the ship."

"Yeah?"

"Proper foreigners," said Rick. "Not Asians.

He thinks they were Russians. And possibly one American.”

“American or English?” Rick translated, and the fishing skipper shrugged his shoulders. “Can he describe him?” Rick translated this, too, and the fishing skipper shrugged again and said something. “What did he say?”

“He said, ‘You all look the same to him’.”

“Why didn’t he tell the authorities?”

“Someone within the authorities would be in on anything which went down. Nothing can happen in China without the authorities knowing.” Rick nodded at the skipper. “He wants cash.” Garnet handed over a sizeable wad and the fishing skipper flicked through it and shrugged, which seemed to be a habit with him. He said something.

“You were just interested in seeing a typical Chinese fishing boat and his nephew kindly brought you over,” said Rick.

Understood,” said Garnet.

As they chugged back, Malcolm turned round to face Garnet and shouted into the wind, “Want a mate’s job? We can’t get anyone to come out here. They don’t want to leave the Riviera.”

“On that thing?” said Garnet. Malcolm smiled.

“Delivery trip. Be an experience.”

XLV

Southern Thailand

The nurse rolled over onto her front and lit up a cigarette. “And my share?” she said. The doctor smiled. “Why are you smiling?”

“What share?”

“You were up to something with those Russians.”

“Be fair.”

“I don’t think...”

"Good, don't think." The nurse rolled over onto her back again and then sat bolt upright and chewed her bottom lip in frustration. "Don't do that. You'll make it bleed. I bought you a gold necklace, didn't I?"

"You had to win."

"I did win."

"You didn't try too hard with those kids and I don't think…"

"I told you. Good that you don't think."

"I don't think the girl was too critical."

"I'm a terrible doctor. I have evidence of this. It's not a crime to be incompetent. What more do you want?" He pointed at her tiny breasts. "Silicon tits?"

"You should sort your wife out with some first."

"She's elegant. Elegant women don't have silicon tits. You're more of a sex doll. For your type, it's practically mandatory."

"You're a bastard." The doctor sighed and sat down and stroked her.

"Listen. You have nothing but a crazy theory and no evidence. People will say you're mad. Anyway, do you know that girl's history? She's the one that all the fuss was made over when she supposedly disappeared. The authorities are sick of her name even. No one is going to want to listen." He flicked the gold necklace and then stroked her breasts. "Be happy with what I've given you. You didn't give it up cheap. Be proud of yourself for that. You don't have to be some kind of…" He stuck his finger into the corner of his mouth. "What is the name of that British literary detective?"

"Sherlock Holmes."

"Yeah, Sherlock Holmes. You don't have to be some kind of Sherlock Holmes."

"I'm not satisfied."

"Well, baby, I don't have any more spunk left in me, so you'll just have to be."

"That's not what I mean and you know…" The girl gave up. The doctor wasn't listening any more.

XLVI

Bangkok

Petunia listened to Crystal. "You know that bitch you don't like."

"I don't not like her; I just don't approve..."

"Yeah, yeah, yeah. Anyway, she's disappeared. Well, she hasn't been in for a long time and no one's seen her. I mean a lot of people are happy she's gone. She was a top girl, lots of very special clients, and they passed her name around. Most of these U.S. digital billionaire types are bi. When they fly in... So, anyway, no one cares, but I just thought you'd want to know. Rumour has it someone slammed your face into a mirror. Was it her? I'll bar her if she did it. If she's ever found, that is, which I don't suppose she will be. You still there, Petunia?"

"Thank you for the information, Crystal."

"A sweetie such as you should not be working in this line, Petunia."

"It's because I'm a sweetie, that I'm successful."

Petunia went straight round to the Anglo Thai and confronted the owner. He frowned as she walked in. "I told you what you wanted to know," he said. "There was a British seaman staying here. He left without his company paying his bill, or paying it himself. There was a ladyboy around... That's all I know."

"There's more." The hotel owner gave her a look which signified that he thought she was insignificant and just an unnecessary bother. Then the Special Victims detective walked in. "Hey," protested the owner. The Special Victims detective just lifted up the little flap in the counter, walked round, grabbed the little man by the throat, and slammed him into the pigeonholes behind him.

"I don't know who they were," squawked the man, fighting to get the air out while he was being choked.

"Let him go," said Petunia and the detective relaxed his grip. He waved his fist in the man's face, causing him to flinch.

"I don't know." The detective menaced him. "They took another sack out. I mean they took one out probably with the British guy's body and then another with the ladyboy later on."

"So, Russians?" The man looked at Petunia, wide-eyed.

"Different ones. I shouldn't be blamed. It's not my fault what goes on in the rooms. People skip on bills. Other people take sacks out. I don't know what's going on. That's not a crime. Ignorance is not a crime."

"You're the captain of this ship," said Petunia. "Everything which happens on board is something for which you can be blamed. Tell me more about the Russians."

"I told you. Brutal-looking guy."

"You said there were Russians plural."

"O.K. The other one was just a skinny, sinister type. He's been here on other occasions."

"Identity?" said the detective.

"Are you kidding?" said the owner. The detective menaced him again. "He pays triple. Who cares about identities?" said the man, spreading out his arms to indicate his exasperation. The detective shot a glance at Petunia. Petunia shrugged.

"You're not off the hook," he said to the little man while still looking at her. The little man brushed himself down.

"O.K., O.K.," he said. "But, please, now that you've forced me to tell you, make sure you catch him before he finds out."

"We will," said the detective. "Thank you for being a good citizen." He performed a mocking little bow.

As soon as they were gone, the hotel owner

let out a long sigh and slumped against the pigeonholes.

XLVII

Bangkok

"I want to go down and poke around, Garnet," said Petunia. "I don't think they died like that. Fish poisoning. I don't believe it." Garnet chewed his fake Bic.

"We were paid to find him, that's all. But this ship thing. He was involved in some ship business. Russians were involved in this Yantau ship business. He appeared, disappeared, appeared, died. Suspicious.

"So?"

"O.K."

Petunia took a look around the town and then appeared in the hospital. The receptionist looked her up and down and said, "By what authority are you here?"

"None."

"So?" Petunia spread her arms wide.

"I'm just satisfying the family's..."

"All right. I suppose I can see if the doctor wants to have this conversation. He's a very nice man.

The doctor came through and looked Petunia up and down, himself, taking in her ladyboy attributes. "Sorry, I don't do that sort of thing," he said with a girlish little giggle. Petunia smiled, sweetly.

"Did you find out what killed them?"

"Of course. Poisonous fish?"

"Which species?"

"Am I under examination by a medical board. This sort of thing is patient privilege."

"There are no patients. They died. In this hospital." Petunia had been on the point of saying,

'Under your care' but had managed to restrain herself.

"If we have an official request for information from the Russian Embassy, we shall provide them with a toxicology report," said the doctor.

"So, you couldn't save either one of them?"

"Evidently."

"This is rare, nowadays, isn't it?" The doctor shrugged.

"It happens." Petunia saw a nurse standing in a doorway behind him and tried to avoid looking at her, but flicked her gaze in her direction, and the nurse mouthed something. The doctor spun round, but the nurse had nipped into a room. He turned back to face Petunia. "I really can't help you, I'm terribly sorry." Petunia smiled.

"Well, thank you, anyway, doctor. You've been most cordial." The doctor waited for her to say something else. She nodded politely at him and then at the receptionist and then left, the doors parting with a swish as she exited the hospital. She hung around outside the entrance, playing with her mobile phone to give her an excuse to remain there for a time, and then the nurse came out and stood next to her and lit up a cigarette. Petunia deliberately avoided looking at her, just pocketing the slip of paper which the nurse surreptitiously passed to her, and then went off in the direction of her hotel.

That night, she rang the mobile number written on the piece of paper, and the nurse said, "The beach road, by the café, twenty minutes."

Petunia wasn't sure if it were the same woman when the nurse turned up. The starched, stiff, health worker now looked like a supermodel. "I hate him," she said, once she was at Petunia's side. "He thinks he is God's gift to women, so smooth. He cheats on his wife. He wants me to have sex with him." She blushed. "That would be illegal in America, wouldn't it? You know. A senior member of staff demanding sex. I think I missed out on a promotion, because I turned him down, but I can't prove it."

"That sort of thing is nearly always impossible to prove." Petunia had quickly worked out that the woman had given in and was now ashamed.

"If I wanted to be a whore, I could go to Pattaya."

"This sort of thing has been going on forever, but I'm not a social worker or a lawyer. I suppose you could get a lawyer if you wanted..." The woman snorted.

"Yeah, sure," she said. "You want to know what went on?"

"I do, of course."

"The embassy staff weren't very aggressive."

"They were here?" Petunia's surprise was evident in her tone of voice."

"I thought you said you were acting for their families. You mean the Embassy isn't involved in your trip here?"

"It's complicated." The nurse pondered this.

"Will I get into trouble?"

"There aren't any guarantees that you won't, but I don't think so." The woman seemed to be considering this. In her mind, her loathing for the doctor was fighting her instinct for self-preservation.

"I thought the girl would recover. She didn't seem to be nearly so ill as the boy. I finished my shift on their last day and went home and then when I came in in the morning, they were both gone. It normally takes a long time for all the formalities to be completed. You know: reports, investigations, arrangements made. They didn't even ask if the families wanted the bodies sent home. They just cremated them. Or so they said."

"How many deaths from fish poisonings have you had in this hospital. The woman looked at Petunia.

"Foreigners? That's what's so suspicious. None. I mean they've had some on the islands, but then the victims were normally so drunk they didn't realise they were ill. At least, that's what I think. I don't want to malign the dead. But once the victims get into a hospital. I mean… these days. With all the modern drugs etc. Are you thinking their families will sue for medical negligence?"

"Medical malpractice, you mean, but no. I am one hundred per-cent confident that that will not happen."

"Is there something more you want?"

"You've told me more than enough."

"You know, I'd love to testify against him. He groped me once. He wants to be a star in the medical profession, but he's a terrible doctor. But I don't think that's why they died, because he didn't seem to be worried. An incompetent doctor who didn't know what he was doing would be panicking, wouldn't he?"

"I would think so."

"So, what happens?"

"I shouldn't mention this conversation to him."

"Oh, I won't. I'd like to transfer to the other hospital, but I'd lose all my benefits. Should I just continue to sleep with him?" She blushed again, realising that she'd blurted out the truth.

"I think you should do what you want to do. Why don't you emigrate to Australia? They always want nurses."

"I didn't bother learning English to a high standard."

"Do a course. It's not difficult. Only if you're dealing with the English themselves, who can't even speak their own language properly, despite the fact that they invented it."

"My parents…"

"Ah, yes. The dutiful Thai girl."

"Someone told me you can take them with you."

"It's difficult. It gets more difficult every year. Listen. I'd buy you dinner, but you shouldn't be seen with me."

"Oh, that's all right."

"Take care."

"You, too." Petunia walked away, plucking her mobile out of her handbag. "Is that a genuine Gucci bag?" said the woman.

"Yes," replied Petunia.

"I could probably have one of them if I were to sleep with him more times. He's generous to his wife and mistresses."

"What good is a handbag if you lose your soul." The woman slumped and turned away to look at the floodlit beach.

XLVIII

Bangkok

Garnet was disappointed. The welder whom the owner of the café had put Petunia onto had disappeared. The yard had only a tug in it now, some tanker having left. He smoked a cigarette and wondered what line of enquiry to pursue.

Once back at the office, he put his feet up on his desk and tipped back his chair, ignoring Petunia's disapproving glance. "it's a piece of junk anyway," he said, laconically.

"There's been another disappearance, Garnet," she said.

"I know Petunia. I was at the yard, remember. You sent me down there."

"Not the welder."

"A related disappearance."

"Well, a seaman."

"Are we playing twenty questions?"

"Your friend."

"Well, that does narrow it down to a sprinkling of people. I like that: a sprinkling of people. If it's anyone from the Union Jack or Shane or anyone connected with him, I hope you don't think they're my friends." He puffed on his cigarette. "Because, they, manifestly, are not."

"Someone else." Garnet rolled his eyes.
"Ronnie," said Petunia.

"Skinny Ronnie?"

"Skinny Ronnie."

"Hmmm. Don't think you could call him a seaman. A seafarer yes. He's a ship's engineer. Anyway, who told you he's missing?"

"Who do you think?"

"Angel. I didn't know you were on familiar terms with her."

"She was in Crystal's. She used to come in there a lot before she hooked up with Ronnie. She likes to be with her own kind when she's not ripping off Westerners on the pool table."

"She doesn't rip them off. She thrashes them. If they're stupid enough to gamble, that's their lookout. So?"

"I asked her what Ronnie's up to and she just said 'working'."

"Ronnie's a barely functioning alcoholic. The only place he could get a job is on some merchant ship and not one owned by someone like B.P., if B.P. even employs British seafarers anymore."

"I just thought. You know. That Johnno is hanging around the yard. Ronnie has disappeared and..."

"And what?"

"Angel said that Ronnie wants to take her to the U.K."

"Ronnie couldn't afford to take her to the cinema."

"Ordinarily not."

"And he won't be making big money at sea. No one has since the sixties. Not unless you're a P and O cruise ship captain or something."

"There's something going on, Garnet. The Russian was a seaman."

"Ship's engineer, too."

"Exactly. That's three ship's engineers disappeared, suddenly."

"You're counting Johnno being around the

shipyard and then not being. Maybe he just went back to Hong Kong." Petunia picked up the phone.

"And that welder who wanted to talk to me but was too frightened," she said. She turned her attention to the receiver and spoke to someone at immigration. "You know Johnno's proper name?" she asked Garnet.

"John Gillespie." She repeated this to her contact and Garnet heard the girl on the other end reply.

"Didn't fly out," translated Petunia.

"Left on a ship?" asked Garnet.

"They don't have information on ship's crew departures at this office. You want her to find out?"

"Sure, why not."

"It costs, and you're paying for all this, aren't you?"

"Would Angel send Ronnie into any danger?" Petunia shrugged.

"She loves him, but she's growing frustrated."

"Her own fault. Should have signed up with a rich Yank, like you did."

"Walt wasn't rich, and I did love him, sort of. I just didn't like living in some Mid-western..."

"Yeah, yeah. All right. I'll pay. Even if it doesn't turn out to be anything to do with Andre's case, I'll find some way to stuff it into his bill. It does some good to throw a bit of cash at the informants occasionally." Petunia spoke into the phone, listened to the girl on the end of the line and then put the receiver down. "She says it'll take a little while."

"Should I go to see Angel? I think I should." Garnet took his feet off the deck, planted them on the floor and pushed his chair back.

"You want me to come?"

"Nah. She won't tell me anything if you're there. I'll look in the bar in which they rip off the punters. If she's not there..."

"Crystal won't let you in her place if she's not in the poolroom and she's gone back there."

"She probably won't have and I know that I, along with all white men, are persona non grata at Crystal's delightful venue."

"All Thai men, too."

"Hmmm."

Angel was sitting in her usual seat in front of her usual pool table. There weren't many people around. Fat Les was demolishing some British kid at another table, using his full repertoire of trick shots, and their table had all the attention. Garnet slid into a seat at Angel's side.

"He's not around," she said, without looking at him.

"I worry about Ronnie," said Garnet.

"I don't, not anymore."

"You're the most luvey-duvey couple in Bangers."

"We were once. Poverty gets boring."

"What's he up to, Angel?"

"You're the detective."

"And his best friend."

"If you'd known, you wouldn't have…"

"Known what and wouldn't have what?"

"Never mind."

"Angel, there's something going on with some ship. There are dead seamen, in China and Thailand."

"Ronnie's a big boy."

"Ronnie's a little kid who wouldn't have a cup of tea without your permission."

"I'm not his mother."

"You're more of a mother to him than his mother ever was."

"Leave it alone, Garnet." The British skinhead with whom Angel had been playing came round the pool table.

"This guy bothering you?" he asked. Angel hissed at him and he went scurrying back to his shot, wielding his pool cue with a bit less bravado. Some other ladyboy laughed at him.

Garnet threw his business card into Angel's

lap. "When it all turns nasty, which it will, don't hesitate to call me, Angel. I know Ronnie wouldn't have gone back to sea if there weren't some big, illicit pay off and he wouldn't have got a job on a proper company. His ticket expired years ago and as for a medical..." He stood up and looked down at her for a little while and then he took comfort from the fact that she didn't throw his card onto the floor. He turned to go. "Good luck," he said to the skinhead, with a smile. The skinhead watched him walk out and wondered if he should start a fight, but decided against it. He was frightened of the ladyboy.

XLIX

Bangkok

The Chinese businessman lay back on his huge bed and searched for the porn channel on the hotel's T.V. system. The maid interrupted him by knocking on the door, handing him a bottle of mineral water and offering to do a turndown. He smiled and said, "Thanks, but no thanks."

He was a very happy man. Thanks to his father' being a senior member of the party, a spell at an American university had been followed with an appointment to a junior role in a fledgling armaments company on the fast track to a senior role, and seeing as the Belt and Roads initiative was, definitely, soon going to be turning into a fighter jets and tanks initiative, he had a very bright future ahead of him. The only fly in the ointment was a taste for serious BDSM practices – just about as serious as they can get – which he'd picked up in San Francisco, during wild, coke-fuelled nights out, on the occasions he felt he could set aside his studies, having done enough for a while to be considered a dutiful son. Apart from one rather nasty occasion when he'd gone to a mixed venue and had a frightening experience in the sauna when an aggressive bear had been enamoured of his hairless, olive-skinned body and had only been frustrated in an attempted rape by the entry into the room of a matronly American woman, he'd had a lot of fun. Unfortunately, being a psychotic would-be rapist himself, he'd found his perverted sexual desires had become an obsession and an addiction. As addicts found with most addictions, he'd constantly had to increase his dosage to achieve the same effect. There had been an incident in China which his father had covered up and which had led to a firm rebuke, but this was Thailand and he was sure his contact would turn up something most satisfying which wouldn't entail any consequences.

The porn channel bored him. It was too vanilla. He switched over to the Bloomberg financial channel to see how his U.S. stocks, bought on the sly with his share in the profits of some start-up he'd assisted with his IQ of a hundred and fifty brain were doing. They were doing spectacularly. More funds. Not much to spend them on, though, when you hated driving, didn't like getting involved in relationships, already owned apartments in Shanghai and London and couldn't possibly consume more cocaine without dying very quickly. There was only his little hobby.

He often wondered what it would have been like to run some prison in Mao's times. It must have been heaven: so many people at your mercy. The disposable mobile which had been left for him at the desk rang and a broad smile appeared upon his rotund face. "Hello," he said.

"I have an opportunity for you."

"I thought you might."

"Western." The Chinaman instantly became very excited.

"Oh, this is too good to be true. White?"

"Whiter than white. A snow princess."

"Russian?" The Chinaman was very excited now.

"Could be."

"Shame you can't get me an American. I love how they squeal just before...

"Shut up you idiot." The Chinaman was a little offended.

"I am a client," he insisted.

"Not for much longer if you're not more circumspect." The Chinaman took a deep breath.

"I wish to apologise for my behaviour. Can we talk in person?"

"There will be photos sent to this phone soon. There's no need for discussions yet. Fifty thousand dollars."

"Fifty thousand for, eh, you know, to completion?"

"Of course. I'm not an amateur."

"Fantastic."

"I thought you'd like it."

"It's just a little expensive."

"O.K., I'm sorry I troubled you. Good luck with some other dealer."

"No, no. The price is O.K. I was only a little surprised. Actually, it's very reasonable. For top quality that is, which I am sure this is."

"O.K., that's better. I'll call you tomorrow with some more details: where and when, that sort of thing."

"Great, great."

"O.K. It's wonderful to be doing business with you, again."

"You're still talking and there's nothing more to discuss right now." The call was cut off. The Chinaman looked at the mobile and then clambered off the soft mattress to place the phone in the bottom of his carry-on bag. He was so excited he could barely restrain himself from singing. He stripped off and went into the steam room, with a massive erection.

L

Bangkok

Shane was in his favourite music bar adjacent to Nana Plaza, listening to a Thai band performing Stairway to Heaven. They had a girl singer who, seemingly confused, combined Led Zeppelin's lyrics with Mick Jagger style prancing. The audience was too wasted to notice the incongruity.

A mild-mannered British pensioner was on a stool at the same table as him and seemed to be transfixed by Shane's facial artwork. He'd had new lip metalwork installed and this combined with his facial tattoos made him look even more frightening than normal. To put the pensioner at ease, he smiled, revealing thousands of dollars-worth of the finest dental work available in Bangkok.

"My daughter has a tattoo," said the pensioner, in an attempt to be convivial.

"On her face?"

"On her bottom, I believe. I've never seen it, of course."

"I should hope not." One of Shane's criminal contacts wandered in and indicated that Shane should join him at another table. Shane rose, and the pensioner flinched. Shane patted him on the head, his hand siding in the sweat in the man's bald patch. "Nice speaking to you," he said. The pensioner looked relieved. Shane sat down with the other man.

"I can't hold a conversation in this din," said the man. He was a burly Brit, not as burly as Shane, but still someone who could clearly look after himself.

"Let's go to my office," said Shane. They went out and across the street to Shane's kebab shop. He told the Turk who worked there to scram and swung the sign round to indicate that the place was closed. "And?"

"There has been something going on. Someone is selling girls, Westerners when he can get them."

"Why buy from him? Elodie has the serious bdsm market sewn up. She runs it well, being an enthusiast herself."

"Elodie?"

"The French Lady."

"She's a dom?"

"Well, she certainly isn't a sub."

"Imagine that. A tiny thing like her. Gets it from her mother, I suppose. That sadistic bitch castrated..."

"Yeah, O.K. Got a name?"

"He calls himself Jeff, or, rather, he has done on occasion. Unlikely to be his real name. He's a wraith. Just appears from time to time. Only deals in white girls with rare exceptions i.e. black girls for Yanks from the Southern States and..."

"And what?"

"As to why the punters with whom he deals don't go to Elodie: he sells them the ultimate kick."

"You're joking. I didn't think,,,"

"I'm not. Exclusive clientele. Got millions. Can afford to buy their way out of anything, either with cash or through their lawyers and the usual Illuminati-style contacts. Some acquaintance of mine from the TBAS listened in on some whispers."

"So, it's true."

"Eh?"

"Never mind." Shane wafted his hand through the fetid air, inviting his associate to continue. "Who's behind him?"

"None of the usual suspects."

"Special Victims know about this?"

"Of course not."

"You know anything of the clients?"

"Yeah, an American. Patrician type. Family came over on the Mayflower etc. etc. Think about it. It's easily deniable, isn't it. You'll never find this Jeff unless you stake out the TBAS and he's only got to come in with a wig on one time and a skinhead cut the next time and..."

"Yeah, yeah. How does he do his communications?"

"Burner phones."

"You need ID in Thailand." The man shrugs.

"Buys them overseas. You don't need ID in Blighty. So, you and the Kiwi going to sort it?"

"Doubt it. It's bad for business, but there's always been someone offering snuff coming along from time to time. It's Elodie's problem. We'll just want to help her find them. Some people are sick, eh? We offer good, clean fun. Elodie offers what the British public-school crowd craves." He raised an eyebrow, quizzically.

"I went to a comprehensive school. They didn't cane us; they just punished us by not teaching us how to read and write. Just an existence." Shane wasn't paying attention. "I don't have any more for you." Shane took the hint.

"Take Clara. Tell Baz I said you get her for the whole night. No bar fine. Tell Clara it's a personal favour to me, so she's not to expect anything more than a small tip and that I'm expecting a good report from you." He handed the man a little notebook and pen. "Write down everything you know about the American." The man quickly complied.

"How did you know I like Clara?" The man was thinking, wistfully, of Clara's dyed-blonde hair framing her olive-skinned face.

"It's my business." The man left, and Shane rapped on the window to let the Turk know that he could open up for business again.

LI

Bangkok

Shane and Garnet met in Garnet's offices for once. Shane looked out of place, but then, Shane looked out of place anywhere. Petunia focussed on some invoices while Shane lit up a cigarette and looked around him. There were photos on the wall of rusty tankers and of Garnet at his passing out ceremony at Hendon police college. "You should have done better in the police, Garnet." Garnet shrugged.

"It's all politics, same as with everything else nowadays. Once they chucked out half the flying squad in the seventies, the officious university graduates took over. The corruption's still there, but you've got to be smooth with it."

"In another life, Garnet, I could have been a police sergeant in Sydney. Do you know they run some of the biggest criminal empires in Australia?" Garnet smiled, at nothing. "O.K.," said Shane, "I'll get to the point. Something's going on." We sort of know who. Some, what was it someone called him, a wraith? Yes, a wraith, organising, or selling, rather, girls."

"This is a development," said Garnet, sarcastically. We're living in Bangkok,"

"For the ultimate thrill."

"Severe BDSM?"

"Garnet."

"Snuff? You serious?" I didn't think..."

"Yeah, it's happening, and, we want to know who's behind it and..."

"You're vanilla, though. This is more a threat to Elodie." Shane looked annoyed and Garnet realised he hadn't liked being interrupted.

"Can you imagine the intrusive investigations the whole scene will be on the end of if this makes it into the media. It's generally bad for business."

"Just lift this "wraith" of the street and torture him."

"And if we find out he's working for someone far more important than us?"

"Got anything to go on?" said Garnet.

"One thing." Shane threw the slip of paper with the frustrated American client's details on it in front of him. "Some customer. And the "wraith" operates out of that society."

"Can you be a little more specific?" Shane's facial tattoos crinkled as a look of annoyance swept over his face.

"That society for bitter foreign divorcees."

"That almost describes the entire expatriate community in Bangkok, but I think I know which you mean."

"You should be divorced, Garnet. It's not fair that you got away. Never fell in love?"

"Too paranoid, Shane. Had one relationship that went on for a while. Foundered on mutual paranoia. She thought I only wanted her for sex and I thought she only wanted me for money. Maybe both us were right. Maybe neither. I want more than just a free weekend in Phuket with Jill for this. I might be stepping on some serious people's toes."

"You'll get it. Put on hold anything else you're dealing with."

"I can't. I've got one other project going and I think I'm getting somewhere."

"Give it up."

"I don't want to and it's my business." Petunia who'd so far remained silent, was staring at them. Shave gave her an annoyed look.

"Tell him, Garnet," she said.

"Don't want to," said Garnet. Shane's facial tattoos crinkled again. "O.K., they might be related. A girl who's involved with one of the people we suspect may be connected to our other thing was supposed to have died in a hospital down South, but almost certainly didn't. She's white and beautiful." He threw a surveillance photo down in front of Shane. "Petunia got this from the security at the hospital. It shows an ambulance, which still displays the signage of a hospital which sold it for scrap a year ago, and the face of one of the three men who drove it in, put something looking like a body in the back, and drove it off. Recognise the dude? Any thoughts on the vehicle?" Shane peered at the photo.

"Elodie uses an ambulance for some operations, usually transporting either her own staff who've been beaten or something or her victims."

"And?"

"The criminal." A look of revelation came over Shane's face.

"That British Thai dude who works for Elodie."

"Exactamente, Shane," said Garnet. Shane looked up at him. "She doesn't know. Unofficial side operation."

"Bit like your kebab shop."

"Garnet, I have my own businesses. The Kiwi doesn't mind."

"I'll work on it."

"If it's the Thai military or something..."

"Unlikely. China, yeah, the military's the biggest mafia. Not here. Someone serious, though. This is why people want to be in the Illuminati, eh? You torture women and kill them and get invited to drinks parties with prime ministers the next day. It appeals to those who just want control. It's the ultimate control isn't it? Control of sex and life. Take what you want without permission. Of course, I mean that's what they want, not ordinary people like us." Shane felt quite complimented being referred to as an ordinary person.

"Just find out who's behind it all." Shane stood up. "Your chairs are too small."

"They're for middle-aged British women, worried about their fathers, husbands or daughters."

"Not their sons?"

"The mothers usually wash their hands of them when they get the letter saying that their little soldier's fallen in love with a ladyboy. It's the fathers who are forgiving You'd think it'd be the other way around, wouldn't you? How's your own family doing?" Shane shrugged.

"Ex-wife's a zombie on OxyContin; daughter's sill in Kong Prem."

"You still trying to get her out."

"Half-heartedly. HIV? Punishment went too far. Every time I go to see her with the lawyer she spits in my face and tells me how much she hates me. She's some British grandma's bitch."

"Prison's not supposed to be nice. That's what an Australian judge said when he sent a pretty boy down who was complaining that whenever he was inside, he got raped."

"Hmmm. Get on it, Garnet." He looked at a photograph on the wall. "Was this your first ship? It's all rusty."

"Yep, taken with the camera my Mum and Dad gave me for my sixteenth birthday. They wanted me to take a photo of every ship I was on. They were very kind people. Skinny Ronnie was on that ship with me. He likes to claim we were both on our first trip. You'd have to be an idiot to believe him. Listen, I think he's involved. I want to keep him out of any complications." Shane was taken aback at this revelation. "On the ship side."

"On the ship side?" Shane shook his head in wonderment. "What ship side? Never mind, Garnet. We don't want Skinny Ronnie. We just want whoever's behind all this." He squeezed himself through the narrow doorway.

LII

Bangkok

Garnet sauntered through the lobby of the five-star hotel. The white-coated staff slid sideways looks at him. It was clear he wasn't a guest - guests didn't wear polyester/cotton-mix suits with linings featuring zombies - but they let him through. He sat down on one of the scarlet, velvet seats which went so nicely with the marble and the mirrors, and waited. Someone came over to him and asked him if he wanted to order something, but he just shook his head.

After a while, a red-faced businessman

appeared from the elevator zone and looked around him. Garnet smiled broadly and waved and the man came over. "What is this?" he said. "Some kind of shakedown? Why didn't you come up to the room?"

"All the rooms in this hotel are bugged," replied Garnet. The businessman looked shocked. "It's the same at the top hotels in London and in your own country."

"You're kidding."

"You think Thailand's security services are any less effective than the U.K.'s or the U.S.A.'s? Think again. Come on. Follow me." Garnet led the way out of the sliding doors, down the ornate steps, and along the broken pavement. "They should make the developers pay for the pavements and the roads, as in Australia. Don't you think? Sorry, sidewalks, not pavements." The American huffed. He followed Garnet into a little café. They were the only customers. Garnet ordered two American coffees in Thai, just to show up the American, and sat down at a table and invited him to join him."

"The deal! What can you tell me?"

"Listen pal."

"Mate, not pal." The American reddened. "It's out. Well, within a very limited circle. Your powerful friends will throw you to the wolves, so don't even bother threatening me. Some very nasty people don't like what'd been going on. It's all right in whatever Eastern European dump 'Hostel' was filmed in, but not in Thailand. It disturbs the Thai authorities and it makes farangs look bad, which is bad for business. Ninety-nine point nine nine nine per-cent of customers just want to have sex with the girls, not kill them. It's not worth the hassle of letting people like whomever is supplying your kind operate."

"This won't..."

"Go any further? Doubt it. Won't get in the media, that's for sure. The Western governments don't want negative stories about Thailand in the media. They're thinking of all those C.I.A. black sites. But there's Twitter, and Facebook, and..."

"I've done it once before."

"Here?" The American nodded. "Don't be embarrassed. Dick Cheney killed half a million with cluster bombs; you've killed one girl. You're both sadists, I'm sure. Still, you won't get a write-up in the Washington Post or whatever."

"I don't know who the supplier is."

"I'm looking for clues. I didn't expect you to provide me with his driver's licence. I know he uses what I believe you call 'burners'. Who put you on to him?"

"Some guy. We were in the same fraternity."

"That's so gay, you know: fraternities. You all live together and have sex with each other. At least that's what always comes up when I accidentally click on the gay section on Xvideos."

"Why doesn't someone just smash your face in?"

"I'm a loveable guy, a misanthrope, but a loveable guy. So, clues, please. Something my friends at Scotland Yard might use to identify him."

"You said you wouldn't..."

"Didn't promise anything. O.K., if you're description is good enough, I'll pick him out myself and let the local mafia do him in. This group?"

"The TBAS."

"The bitches all shat on us? No that would be TBASOU." A look of disgust passed over the American's face at Garnet's language, which made Garnet giggle. The waitress brought their coffees. She said something to the American. "She wants to know if you want sugar," explained Garnet. The American nodded and she brought over a bowl.

"Skinny guy. Thirty-odd. Chain smokes. Grey-faced. Looks like he did time. Bad teeth. Medium height"

"American."

"I said bad teeth, didn't I? English."

"That's a little bit offensive, but never mind. I'll overlook it. How often does he go to this gathering of whingers?"

"On Thursdays. It's only held on Tuesdays and Thursdays, anyway."

"Nice suit. Don't go for grey, myself. Sammy or Raja?" The American was irritated at this jocularity.

"Saville Row."

"Yeah? Nice. Garnet felt the lapel. Superfine. Ten grand?"

"Six."

"Sammy would have done it for a thousand." Garnet pulled out the flap of his suit to display the lining. "He made this. Like it?"

"It's great," said the American, sarcastically.

"Something more."

"What?"

"Something more. I want something exceptional. Some information."

"I think he's moving into political or commercial blackmail. Dumped me out of a deal on the new girl he's bringing in and said I shouldn't be offended because it wasn't about money."

"Go home. Don't come to Thailand again. Think yourself lucky to get away with even thinking of doing this again in Thailand. Find some teenage runaway in some dirt-poor U.S. state to do your thing with." The American stood up. "Just a minute."

"What?" said the American.

"What does TBAS stand for?" The American smiled.

"You'll find out, you sick bastard." He turned and left.

"Pot, kettle, black," said Garnet quietly. "And don't offer to pay for the coffees, either, you tight git."

LIII

On the ship. Bay of Bengal

Johnno had Ronnie by the throat and was

squeezing. The vicious look on his face was a sign that there would be no mercy. Suddenly, someone grabbed him and spun him round. It was the Russian, "Listen," said the big man, face held inches from that of a wide-eyed Johnno, "you couldn't do the job. He's making you a fool, yes, but you couldn't do the job." Ronnie, himself, was too out of it to say anything. He didn't even have the energy to raise his hands to his neck and rub it. "We sort this out when we arrive," the Russian continued. Johnno sneered and wandered off, and the Russian gave Ronnie a sympathetic look.

"Try not to make him look stupid, eh?" Ronnie nodded. He wished Angel were here to stick a shiv in Johnno's stomach. "You didn't want to come, so we got Johnno, and now it's easier to take him with us than dump him, you understand?" Ronnie nodded.

"It was electrical," he said. "He's useless at electrical."

"He is Australian, yes?" Ronnie nodded again. "You are almost the same. Why don't you get on?"

"All the English who couldn't get on with anyone were dumped in Australia."

"Ah. It was like a gulag?"

"A sunny one." The Russian looked over the railing at the main engines, pounding away.

"I love steam engines," he said.

"They're two-stroke diesels." The Russian shrugged. "I will kill Johnno, if you like, once we arrive." Ronnie shook his head. "Ah," said the Russian. "You are too soft. Our employer is not happy with him. He said he could do the job and then he couldn't. That's not fair.

"What happened to the original engineer, truly?" The Russian gave him a wry smile.

"Don't be frightened."

"Is he alive?" The Russian smiled. He patted Ronnie on the head.

"I like you, Englishman," he said. "You're a nice guy. Not like that other one." He nodded in the direction in which Johnno had gone. "Him, I do not like."

"Give me a cigarette." The Russian handed him one of his own favourite brand. Any normal Western smoker would have coughed upon inhaling from it, but Ronnie, whose lungs were mostly solid tar, just sucked the smoke down greedily His eyes seemed to water a little, though.

"I like that girl who brought you in the car," said the Russian. Tell him it was a man and you're dead, Ronnie thought. The Russian slapped him on the back, making him cough, violently. "I am kidding. I know it wasn't a woman. We have the same humour, eh, us and you British? Tell me, why do you hate us?"

"We don't hate you," said Ronnie, breathlessly. "We just think you're crazy and dangerous. Anyway, any nation which defeated the Germans twice and Napoleon can't be all bad."

"Ah, General Kutuzov. Brilliant guy. 'You want Moscow. Take it. Then try to get home after we have burnt all out own villages and destroyed the crops. You will starve. A genius."

"Yeah, him. How will we get home, after...?" The Russian patted Ronnie on the head again.

"You worry too much. Always thinking of tomorrow. Be like our friend Johnno. Just worry about today. Seriously, I think I shall kill this Johnno. I think he is a bully. A school bully. But we are not in school now, are we?" Ronnie realised the man was waiting for an answer.

"More like on job experience," he said.

"Thank you for fixing that fault on the generator."

"My job," replied Ronnie with a shrug.

"If I receive permission to kill this Johnno, then you shall receive his share. It is only fair. We Russians are very fair. You know how many stolen ships this Bangladeshi has bought? Seven. No one is policing this."

"IMO." The Russian spat on the floorplates.

"Bureaucrats. In Russia we know what to do with them."

"Siberia?" The Russian slapped him on the back.

"Siberia. Yes, Good joke. Continue with your work. This Johnno shall not bother you again today." The big man walked away, along the gallery. Ronnie sighed and slumped against the railings.

LIV

Bangkok

Garnet slipped into the divorced and separated men's club, which was in one half of the basement of a third-rate hotel in Sukhumvit. Some kind of Japanese hostess dancing club was in the other half, and the two streams of attendees to the Thursday nights events entered through the hotel doors without seeming to notice each other, even filing off to different staircases despite the fact that both staircases came together again at the basement level.

A skinny Englishman in a Harrington jacket was bemoaning his ex-wife's spite from the lectern. Murmurs of agreement and outrage circulated around the crowd. After a while, the speaker broke down in tears and mumbled that it was time for Bernie to take over again. A big, guy, who, unlike all the other members, looked quite happy, bounced onto the stage and said, "Let's all give Matthew a round of applause," the words being a bit muffled as they had to pass through his bushy black beard.

Garnet looked around him. He couldn't see anyone fitting the dealer's description, but it was early yet. "Hey," he said to the man next to him. "What does TBAS stand for."

"Ted Bundy Appreciation Society," said the man. Garnet's jaw hung down.

"What?"

"Ted Bundy Appreciation Society." The man was irritated and didn't want to be bothered with Garnet; he wanted to listen to Bernie. Garnet, still a little shocked, continued to look around him for the dealer. After a while, he saw someone who fit the description slink in. Middle-age or even old age, having affected most of the attendees, the lights were up bright so they wouldn't have to strain to see and Garnet saw the same look on the man's face that he had seen on other evil psychopaths of his acquaintance: the few he'd met on tankers and the many he'd met during his time in the Metropolitan Police, among both the villains whom he'd been chasing and the officers with whom he'd been working.

Bernie stomped off the stage, handing the mic over to another bitter individual. Garnet didn't know what they were moaning about. Their wives had booted them out, stolen their homes, cars and pensions, living them no choice but to retire to Bangkok where their pittances, left them by flinty-eyed judges, were enough to survive on. Then, instead of living in some mind-numbing suburb with a woman whom they didn't particularly like, they were living like teenagers let loose in a brothel. Garnet pinned down Bernie.

"Hi," he said.

"You're recently divorced; you've just arrived, and you want to join a supportive community."

"Eh, yeah," said Garnet.

"Wrong!" said Bernie. "You're Garnet, the detective, either the cuckold's best friend or a parasite."

"Maybe both," said Garnet.

"What do you want?"

"Why's the nickname the Ted Bundy Appreciation Society?"

"Sometimes people are bitter, you know."

"He killed women, and raped them."

"Like I said. Anyway, allegedly."

"He was convicted."

"By an American court."

"Yeah of thirty-three murders. Even with a substantial error rate, I think he was still guilty of the majority of them. Anyway, if he didn't do it, why would you admire him? It's illogical. You admire him because you think he did do it and you're all women haters." Bernie shrugged. "Anyway, why not the Peter Sutcliff Society?"

"That'd be a bit sick, wouldn't it?" Garnet just stared at him." "And Sutcliff murdered working girls. We like working girls."

"Bundy's victims didn't have time to take any men to the cleaners in the divorced courts, eh? They were all college students. Anyway, just because he was played by a Disney actor... He wasn't a Disney character, you know?"

"Look, what do you want? Are you from the Women's Liberation Society or something?"

"No, I'm just a detective, like you said. There's been something going on out of your club."

"Oh yeah."

"Something hideous."

"Gay thing?" Garnet was surprised again.

"You must be the most politically incorrect person on the planet."

"I'm the king. This is my kingdom. I started this club."

"Listen, I'd bury that nickname if I were you. It might look as though you were encouraging that sort of thing."

"Who's operating out of my club?"

"I'm not telling you that. I'm just fishing. Seeing if you know anything."

"How do you expect any information if you won't tell me whom you want information on. It's not something involving kids, is it?"

"No. At least I don't think so. All right, but don't approach him. That guy over there. The weaselly-looking one."

"Can you be more specific. They're all

weaselly-looking.”

"Don't have a very high opinion of your members, do you? Brown leather jacket.”

"Jeff.”

"You have membership records.”

"Yeah. You don't get in after the free look-around if you're not a member.”

"Will you give me his address? You're going to go down if they think you're involved in his business. Let me be the one who sorts it and I'll make sure the authorities know you were nothing to do with it. You want to keep your little kingdom, don't you? You don't want to be just another sad individual, drinking with the second-rate hookers at ten in the morning, waiting for your turn with the photocopies of the British newspapers.” Bernie scowled and flicked through some documents on his mobile and did a screen shot. What's your number?” Garnet told him. "Wattsapped it to you. Good luck. I got to do my motivation talk now.”

"What are you wanting to motivate them to do?”

"'Happiness is the best revenge'. Seneca said that.”

"I think he put it a bit more elegantly, but yeah. Your version is succinct.”

LV

Outside Bangkok

Petunia found the welder at home.

"So, you've reappeared?” she said, once he'd opened the screen door.

"I didn't want to talk to you,” he replied. "It's dangerous.”

"Come on. Just give me a hint.”

"They've gone now, I suppose.” The welder signalled that she should enter and she followed him inside and they sat down in the poorly furnished living room of his tiny apartment. "That is a bad guy," he said.

"Who?"

"The Australian."

"His name's Johnno. Why did you run away, though? Why did he come out and look?" The man's wife came in with a tray of tea. She showed no surprise at having a ladyboy in her front room. Petunia thanked her politely and made a big effort to sip her tea in a ladylike manner so as to be as unobtrusive as possible.

"They knew I knew."

"Knew what?"

"There was a tanker here. It's sailing with a different name. I saw it in Singapore under its real name."

"Ships change their names all the time."

"They'd tried to hide something. The original name is usually welded on so it's easy to repaint."

"And."

"They'd ground off the original welded name and put a new old welded name on it, i.e. not the same name as the one to which they'd changed it. They did that to hide the original identity of the boat. I could tell."

"Didn't you ask the crew about it?"

"Of course not. There's no good reason to do something like this. Only criminals would do this."

"Did you know that this ship was supposed to have disappeared after leaving China?"

"I suspected something like that after I saw this. They do that, you know. Steal ships. Sometimes they kill the crew, but not this time, not all of them, anyway. I recognised some of them from Singapore. Maybe they recognised me. Maybe that's why they were suspicious. Maybe they just didn't like it when they saw me looking at the welding."

"I'll find out where the ship is going."

"Don't bother."

"And why shouldn't I."

"It's officially going to Saudi, but it's going to Bangladesh. I overheard some of the crew speaking Mandarin. My grandfather was Chinese I understand some of the language."

"What's an empty tanker doing going to Bangladesh?"

"Ships' graveyard. Like in that old Tarzan movie with the elephants' graveyard. Place where ships go to die." He leant forwards, his chin jutting out, for emphasis. "Shipbreakers. He sat back. "I was worried.

"I don't think they'll kill you. Don't worry."

"I wasn't that worried."

"Don't be even a little bit worried. We'll sort this out." Petunia could see the man was frightened.

LVI

Bangkok

Garnet was on the phone to Andre.

"Wire transfer, please. Job done. Time to pay up, my fat, apartheid-supporting friend."

"Garnet, my parents were Welsh and I never supported apartheid and I'm not even from South Africa."

"O.K., from one of those dinky, little, semi-independent republics then."

"What do you want, Garnet? You've really found out what happened to our ship?"

"Sort of. Can't prove it yet, of course. It's on its way to Bangladesh, empty"

"Stolen for scrap?"

"That's a disgraceful slur on the nation of Bangladesh: assuming that's the only reason an empty tanker would be going there, but, yeah, I think so."

"Who steals a ship for scrap?"

"It's a good idea. Like Brinks Mat without the

gold. Low profile.”

"Eh?”

“Brinks Mat. They went in after three and a half million in cash, found twenty-six million in gold and couldn’t resist it. If they’d only taken the cash and walked out, it would have been so low profile that it wouldn’t have even stayed in the papers for more than a day, and the police would have thought they’d got off lightly and just been grateful that the villains hadn’t made fools of everyone. As it was, it’s still in the papers thirty years later and twenty people involved have died or served long sentences or both. What you going to do about this? Sometimes you just keep quiet about these things, don’t you, you Illuminati dudes?”

“I need evidence.”

“Then?”

“We’ll get nowhere with the Bangladeshi authorities, probably, but I need evidence.”

“Send someone then.”

“I’m thinking.”

“Think faster.”

“I’m thinking of sending you.”

“I’ve found out...”

“You’ve not completed the assignment. You haven’t found any evidence. You just have a few rumours. Go to Bangladesh. Find out what breaker’s yard it’s in and send me the pictures.”

“It’s not so much yards. It’s a beach.”

“O.K., find out which beach spot and send me the pictures.”

“So, I don’t get paid until I do?”

“I’ll wire you some more money for expenses. That’s it.”

“You’re a lot more difficult to deal with than suspicious British pensioners who want me to suss out their Thai paramours.”

“I’m a businessman. Listen, you’re Mr Everyman. No one ever pays any attention to you. Even in Bangladesh, you won’t stick out. You’re a nonentity. That’s the whole foundation of your little detective agency. The only reason anyone ever pays any attention to you is that you employ a ladyboy assistant. I'm starting to wonder, Garnet..."

"All right, all right. I'll go. You still haven't bothered thanking me for getting you through your exams."

"Would you like a formal thankyou now?"

"Don't bother. How's your father? I liked him. We shared a passion for red light districts."

"Had some heart trouble."

"I'm sorry to hear that.

"Oh, he's all right. Jumped the NHS queue. There's a regulation that if you have a medical emergency airside in Britain, you get immediate attention in hospital. Booked a ten-pound EasyJet ticket, went through security, lay down on the floor, said, "Oh, my heart", and got his valves done next day."

"He's a smart cookie."

"Good luck, Garnet. Try not to get yourself killed, O.K. It'll be a big payoff. Don't worry."

LVII

Bangkok

Petunia slipped into the Kiwi's Bentley. The Kiwi looked at her askance. Shane, twisting his neck so he could look round from the front passenger seat, was amused.

"Garnet?" said the Kiwi.

"Looking into something else." The Kiwi gave her a fixed stare, and she shrugged. "You're not our only client, you know. Is this an anti-ladyboy thing? Because that would really be a downer." Shane giggled, and Petunia smiled.

"So?" said the Kiwi, resigning himself to dealing with her.

"The guy's definitely working out of that

women-haters' group. We've got someone sat outside his house, someone Thai and unobtrusive. Eventually, he'll go to wherever he's got this Russian girl. He went to see the Chinese guy yesterday afternoon. The Chinese guy is hopping with excitement." The Kiwi mused upon this.

"It's not every day you get to torture a beautiful girl and then kill her."

"He's really a gentle soul," said Shane, indicating the Kiwi. "What's Garnet working on? Go on, tell us?"

"Just tell us if it's related," said the Kiwi.

"It's tangential." Both the Kiwi and Shane raised their eyebrows.

"Big word," said the Kiwi.

"One of Walt's favourites." They looked confused. "My ex-husband's."

"Ah. Didn't like the States?"

"He was from the Mid-West."

"Not ladyboy territory."

"Exactly. The Baptist minister asked Walt to bring his new wife to a service and then nearly had a heart attack when he did."

"In the States, you could have been charged with murder over that. Two news helicopters crashed once while following a police chase and they tried the fugitive for the third-degree murder."

"Soon, this Jeff will take the Chinaman to Ludmilla."

"The Russian girl," said Shane. The Kiwi looked annoyed. Petunia could see that he was thinking, "Obviously, the Russian girl' and was fighting the desire to comment on Shane's tendency to' state the bleeding obvious', as Garnet would have put it.

"So, you still don't know who's behind this Jeff. This is frustrating. We still can't just pick him up and torture him for the information. It could be someone with influence. To be honest, I wouldn't care, but that's not what Elodie wants and I can do without having that psychopathic bitch on my back."

"She doesn't like being called Elodie," said Petunia. "Only her father's supposed to call her that. I don't know how she can let things deteriorate to the stage where one of her own staff is moonlighting with something like this." The Kiwi's jaw hung open.

"What?"

"Didn't Shane pass that on?"

"No, he did not." The Kiwi glared at him. Shane shrugged as if to say 'slipped my mind'.

"That Thai with the British accent who works for her."

"Colin?" Petunia shrugged. "I want to see him skinned alive," said the Kiwi.

"We still don't know who's behind him?" said Shane. "No one would freelance on the French Lady's time without some protection if it all goes…"

"Tits up," suggested Petunia.

"A refined lady such as yourself should not be picking up this gutter language from a lowlife such as Garnet," commented the Kiwi.

"Pete Tong then."

"What?" said Shane.

"Pete Tong. It's Cockney rhyming slang. Pete Tong. Wrong." The Kiwi shook his head.

"Whatever. Thank you for the update."

"Will you tell the French Lady about Colin?"

"I'll have to pick my moment. I need her to stay calm so we can sweep the whole thing up, not have Mr Chang slice him up with a meat cleaver."

"She feeds her victims to the fish in the canal. Imagine that. Sitting on your balcony, having a smoke, slinging bits of human being over the railings, listening to it plop."

"Yes, thank you, Shane," said the Kiwi. He leaned across Petunia and opened her door. "Thank you for your time. I hope Mr Garnet hasn't got himself involved in more than he can handle. He is, occasionally, useful." Petunia smiled at him and slipped out and stood on the sidewalk in Sukhumvit watching the Panzer tank of a car turn round, causing several moped riders to pull emergency stops and one to fall off his bike and slide along the ground. Petunia glanced down at him. He looked all right. He got up, dusted himself off and continued on his way.

LVIII

On a flight over Burma

Garnet sat on the plane with Angel. They weren't sure what kind of reception immigration at Dhaka would give her, Bangladesh being a Muslim country, but it was worth a shot. She wanted to be there. She'd suddenly given in to Garnet's entreaties to take this seriously. Garnet suspected that somehow Ronnie had been able to get in touch.

Skinny Ronald had indeed been in touch and Angel was slightly worried, worried enough, anyway, to listen to Garnet. They'd been the customary assurances that they would both be 'sorted' and he'd told her he would see that Ronnie got his cash. He would dearly love to speak to Ronnie, himself. He wondered if he would get the chance prior to the showdown. The sort of people who stole ships tended to shoot witnesses and co-conspirators. There was little enough chance of a criminal prosecution in anything at sea, apart from the slinging in jail of British captains whose ships had come to grief as a result of some decision by a ruthless superintendent sitting in his office in London. Legality at sea was a grey area. It was a realm in which even cruise-ship rapes were quietly buried.

Garnet had never been to Bangladesh and viewed it as a little mound of sand constantly under threat of being swept away. He gazed out of the window on the odd occasion when there was no cute Thai stewardess in the aisle to ogle.

"I love him, you know. Everyone thinks I don't, but I do." Garnet turned away from the view out of the window to stare at Angel's angular face.

"I believe you," he said.

"You are being sarcastic."

"No, I'm not. You can tell when I'm trying to be funny. I do make my fake, little laugh."

"They won't hurt him, will they?" Garnet had no idea.

"I don't think so," he said. He wondered whether to put the question that'd been bothering him for a while. He decided to go for it. "Why Ronnie?"

"He is a top ship's engineer, or was."

"No, I mean why you and Ronnie? Don't say 'he needs me'. Half the expatriate population of Bangkok needs you or someone like you."

"He is so gentle. There is no harm in him. What was he like when he was younger? You knew him then, Garnet."

"I've known him thirty years." Garnet thought about it. "He was beautiful," he said. "Sometimes it breaks my heart to see what life did to him. Well, alcohol. That was the merchant navy. In those days if you didn't get pissed in the officers' bar every night, you were ostracised." He considered the word and decided that it probably wasn't in her English vocabulary. "No one would..."

"I know what you mean. That killed him, didn't it? It killed his soul." Garnet shrugged.

"Lots of people die inside while their bodies go on living. Bangkok wouldn't have half its foreign population if they didn't. Don't worry, Angel. There are some high-powered people with lots of connections interested in seeing where this all goes. I'm supposed to do things on the quiet, but if it gets too risky, I'll just blow the whistle and call in the cavalry."

"Is Bangladesh nice?" said Angel, dreamily.

"I don't think so, but let's not judge it before we've seen it. Beautiful beaches with tankers stranded on them instead of Holiday Inns and fat tourists. I don't know if that's better or worse. Better,

I think. At least it's something genuine.

LIX

Bangkok

The boy whom Garnet and Petunia had got out of Klong Prem for assisting them in a previous case, with the help of their Special Victims contact, sat outside the procurer's apartment, astride his little motorbike, puffing away on a cheroot. This was fun. He was a star in his little community of waifs and strays, known as the man upon whom the farangs depended to sort out their most important criminal cases. Of course, the foreigners took care of the paperwork, but when it came to the heavy stuff, the nitty gritty, it was him upon whom they relied. The standard of women he was banging had risen remarkably. His mother was happy with him. The sergeant in Special Victims had told him, "Don't think you've *carte blanche*," but he had taken this as just a friendly piece of advice from one colleague to another. He flung the cheroot onto the road and stamped it out, much to the chagrin of an old homeless man in front of whom he did it.

Jeff appeared and summoned a motorcycle taxi and jumped onto the pillion. The bike sped away and Garnet's solitary trainee followed. They weaved their way through a succession of backstreets and the taxi bike pulled up outside a derelict building. Garnet's boy rode on past, turned a corner, parked up, and sidled back. He tried the door through which the man had gone. It was open and he ventured inside. A concrete staircase led to a basement and he descended it and then he faced a steal door. He looked around him and saw a little hidey hole and scrunched himself into it.

After a while, Jeff came out, whistling, and slammed the door behind him. He went up the stairs without looking around him, and, after a minute, the boy slipped out of the shadows and tried the door. It was locked. He quickly pulled out a set of skeleton keys and picked the lock and swung the door open.

There was a solitary lightbulb hanging on a bare cord in a corner and a woman lying beneath it. The boy went over to her. She was in a BDSM harness, her breasts exposed. His gaze lingered on her pink nipples and then he looked into her frightened eyes. He smiled, and she shrank back.

"Ha," he said. "I am one of the good guys."

"I don't believe you," she replied. He laughed.

"It's true. I am saved. I was a convict. I am a born-again Christian now and I work for the law."

"Untie me."

"Not authorised, I'm afraid. Us detectives like to wrap up the whole thing. We're not ready to do that, yet."

"They want to kill me."

"Yes, slowly, and painfully."

"Please, my name is Ludmilla. Please, help me."

"All in good time." The boy liked that phrase. Garnet used it sometimes and he was under the illusion that Garnet came from the upper echelons of British society and thus should be imitated as much as possible.

"They will come and kill me while you are away."

"Nyet. You like that? Nyet. You see, I speak Russian. I and my associates (he was referring to his loose confederation of street kids) will maintain a constant watch upon the building. You have very nice breasts." The girl quickly tried to cover them up, but the restraints prevented her from doing this.

"If you untie me, I will have sex with you."

"Hmmm. I'm afraid that my loyalty to my employer trumps that. Do you like that word 'trump'? It's nothing to do with President Trump. It's from a card game. Petunia gave me lots of books on English idioms."

"Petunia?"

"My associate. Anyway, I must go. Do not worry. I will double up the guard when the sleepy members of my team are on watch." Ludmilla started crying. "Don't do that. There's nothing a sadist likes more than tears. Well, perhaps begging." He noticed a dark patch in the corner and figured it was blood, but he didn't mention his suspicions to Ludmilla. "Oh, one thing, Jeff might make another visit on his own before he brings his customer. Jeff's the name of your captor. Did you know that? Never mind. If Jeff finds out I have been here, he will kill you, instantly, so don't tell him. O.K.? I must go now. As soon as a member of my team arrives, I have to do some shopping for my mother. Is your mother demanding? Mine is very demanding. Sometimes I think I preferred living in prison to living with her. Good luck. At least it's nice and cool down here. It's very hot in the streets." He moved over to the exit. Just before he went out, he gave her a little wave and an encouraging smile.

"You bastard!" she screamed at the door as soon as it had clanged shut.

LX

Bangkok

On the third night, Garnet's boy, on watch with one of his sleepy mates, saw Jeff exit the basement and followed him on the pillion of another bike until they arrived at a little eatery, far away from the main drag. They parked their motorcycle further along the street and hung around, smoking cigarettes and listening to a tinny-sounding radio, until they saw another farang appear. They didn't do anything obtrusive such as taking photographs, but tried to note everything pertinent to the new arrival: clothes, posture, facial features, hair, and then left.

The motorcycle rider dropped the boy off outside Garnet's offices around the corner from Soi Cowboy and the boy went inside, noticing that there was a slight upturn in the quality of the girls waiving massage menus at passing tourists.

Sitting opposite Petunia, he went to light another cheroot.

"Only Garnet smokes in here," she said. The boy shrugged and slid the cheroot back into the packet. He launched into a long description of the visitor. Petunia listened impassively.

"Any thoughts?" he said. Petunia bit her lip. Should she tell him. "Come on. I should know whom I'm tracking. It might be dangerous."

"Sounds like someone we know," she replied.

"And?" She considered this.

"British Intelligence." The boy laughed.

"There's such an organisation. Sounds like a contradiction in terms. Seriously. Friend of yours? Conflict of interest?"

"Not a friend of ours."

"Want me to provide any special services?"

"I don't think so. Not at the moment, anyway." The boy shifted with feigned embarrassment.

"Garnet said he'd pay bonuses for good work."

"Garnet's away."

"Yeah, in Bangladesh."

"How do you know that?"

"Never mind. Just be grateful that your trainee is intelligent and informed and well-connected."

"You're supposed to be following those whom we want you to follow, not us."

"I didn't follow him; it just takes a phone call."

"Garnet's a man of his word. He wouldn't last five minutes in this business if he weren't."

"O.K. You should steer clear of intelligence people, you know. The rules don't apply to them."

"I'm sure Garnet will be grateful for your advice." The boy pondered this. "Listen, he got you out of Klong Prem."

"All right, all right." The boy rose, and Petunia dug into her desk drawer and slung him five thousand baht.

"A sign of good faith," she said. The boy picked it up.

"You're the reason he's successful, you know. Everyone likes you; no one likes him, well, only those other British deadbeats at the Union Jack."

"He's your employer." She looked into his eyes and saw a flicker of fear. "Keep watching the basement."

"I will." He turned to leave.

"Just a minute." The boy paused, with his hand on the door handle.

"You're a good worker. Best thing he's done for this firm is hiring you." The boy considered this, and then left. Petunia called someone on her mobile.

LXI

Bangkok

Petunia sat squeezed on the back seat of the French Lady's Mercedes, between the Kiwi and the French Lady. Chan, Elodie's ape-like bodyguard, had also climbed in, hence the discomfort in the normally ample passenger compartment of the leviathan of an automobile. Shane sat in the front passenger seat.

"And?" said the Kiwi, in his customary stress-free tones.

"The third secretary."

"Whose third secretary?"

"The third secretary. The British one."

"That bastard," said Shane. He snubbed me at a reception at the Aussie Embassy. Just because I have facial tattoos..."

"Shane," said the Kiwi, with a sigh.

"Sorry boss." Shane looked at Petunia. "I get a little bit insecure. I'm easy to offend." The French lady was annoyed.

"Steady on, Elodie," said the Kiwi.

"I've told you not to call me that."

"Things run smoothly when you're in charge, Petunia. I don't know why you don't ditch that little git and set yourself up on your own. If it's capital you need?" Petunia twisted round to look at the Kiwi.

"I'm quite happy with my situation."

"We have to deal with this," said the French Lady.

"We can't take out a British intelligence agent," said the Kiwi. "Even our own side would get annoyed with that."

"The Kiwis have an intelligence agency?" said Shane.

"I was referring to ASIO," said the Kiwi, "and don't raise your eyebrows like that; it screws up your tattoos and makes you look even more disconcerting."

"Don't have any eyebrows," said Shane, quietly.

"Garnet will handle it," said Garnet.

"You handle it, Petunia," said the Kiwi.

"I agree," said the French Lady.

"It's a British affair," protested Petunia.

"It's a Thai and international business community affair," said the Kiwi. "Whom are they setting up? That American went home, so something's changed."

"People who mess with British intelligence disappear."

"People who mess with us disappear," said Shane. "People who mess with Elodie get chopped up into little bits and fed to the fish." The French Lady looked even more annoyed. "Why did you bring Chan? You can trust us."

"Why did our friend bring you?"

"No infighting," said the Kiwi, putting his foot

down. "This affair is a community issue."

"Frighten him off now, and we don't have anything," said the French Lady.

"That's true," said the Kiwi, "and we don't know if he's acting alone or for MI6." The French Lady scoffed.

"They wouldn't want him involved in something sexual."

"Oh yeah, ask that British parliamentarian who moaned about arms trading and was found trussed up in lingerie with an orange in his mouth." The French Lady looked at the Kiwi.

"Is that true?"

"Of course, it's true. Have you ever known me crack a joke? You handle it Petunia. I don't want to wait for Garnet. You can't communicate with him can you, or he'd be joining us on speaker phone."

"Not can't, shouldn't."

"Let's go, Shane." The Kiwi motioned to Chan to get out of the way and, once he'd received the nod from the French Lady, the lumbering giant opened the door and let him out. Shane joined the Kiwi on the side of the road and they watched the Mercedes roll away down the street.

"600 W100. Dictator's car. Could have a nice Bentley like you. The woman's mad. You think Petunia can sort this out on her own?"

"She'll use Special Victims, but that's all right. This happens once in a while. Someone shakes things up; it gets sorted out; things get back to normal."

"O.K., boss."

LXII

Bangladesh, Chittagong

The ship shuddered as it hit the beach at full speed, the pilot breathing a sigh of relief. The pilots operating here were some of the most skilled in the world. One hundred yards out and you were on someone else's patch and had to share the profit.

Johnno stomped around; Skinny Ronald shrank into a corner; the Russian stood as if on parade; the Chinese and Filipinos wondered if they would fly home soon.

Once ladders had been put in position, Alexander was brought on board by the yard owner, who had his little son at his side.

"Good job," said Alexander, to no one in particular. His man thanked him in Russian. Johnno had his non-smile on his face.

"They're going to kill us," aid Ronnie, and Johnno hissed at him. Alexander's expression didn't change. His deputy looked from Johnno to Ronnie, smiling. The yard owner went out onto the bridge wing and looked over. He came back into the wheelhouse and placed the attaché case he'd been carrying upon the chart table. Alexander moved over to it and shoved him out of the way and clicked the clasps and flipped up the lid. Two hundred and fifty thousand U.S. dollars lay inside. Just then the bridge door to the stairwell clanged open and Roman appeared, followed by Garnet and Angel. Ronnie gasped. Alexander's cheeks were afflicted with a faint tinge.

"Ramon!"

"Alexander." Alexander looked at the yard owner with confusion. "You're a traitor, Sasha," continued Ramon.

"It's private business."

"First your brother and now you."

"My brother just had a big mouth."

"Too big, running on and on about the Kursk and the Losharik."

"I killed him."

"You sold the girl."

"British intelligence..."

"Found out and blackmailed you. They were in Yantau, weren't they, or, at least, the third secretary from their Bangkok Embassy? You sold them, or him, Ludmilla for his silence." Smirnov blanched. "We're not even going to bother getting you back to Russia to torture you." Ramon produced a pistol and pointed it at Smirnov's heart.

"My family?" said the potential murder victim.

"They'll be taken care off." Smirnov let out a sigh.

"Thank you."

"Not in a good way, Sasha." Smirnov opened his mouth to protest and the gun roared and he collapsed. The breakers' owner went over to him and tutted at the blood spilling out onto the bridge floor.

"This is a very old ship," he said. "Some of this wood had some value."

Johnno bolted for the door and tore down the stairwell. Garnet wandered out to the bridge wing and looked over and saw him scrambling down the ladder and then running along the beach. "Go on, run away, just like your troops at Singapore. Even your own general ran away," shouted Garnet. Johnno hadn't gone far when a Bangladeshi stepped out from behind a hut and blew his brains out. "That was satisfying," said Garnet. "I'm sure everyone at the Union Jack will breathe a huge sigh of relief." He dialled Andre's number on his mobile.

"Yes, Garnet?" there was a trace of irritation.

"Done it. Found your ship."

"And?"

"It's on the beach in Bangladesh. A breaker's yard. It arrived. I'll send photos."

"How long's it been there?"

"Fifteen minutes."

"You bastard. You were there in time. You let them run it up."

"Listen, what's done is done. You're still going to have to pay out on the claim. The intelligence services are mixed up in this, plus no one is going to want you upsetting the Bangladeshis and whomever was paid off in China, out of spite, so just keep quiet."

"You can forget your fee, you bastard."

"Oh yeah? You want to get a call from the house on the river. Payment in full." There was a pause.

"I have to verify it."

"You think I'd make something like this up?"

"You bastard." Andre hung up, and Garnet went back inside. Ronnie was clinging to Angel. Ramon was rifling through the cash.

"It's all there," said the Bangladeshi. His son hadn't learnt yet to hide his feelings and was clearly offended and was frowning. Ramon looked down at the little boy and patted him on his head.

"Just a minute," said Garnet.

"I agreed to let your friend live, Garnet. Just be grateful for that."

"He wants to be paid," said Angel.

"I sorted out the insurers for you," said Garnet. "I obtained the agreement. You'll still have enough for a new Mercedes." Ramon laughed.

"This money doesn't get spent on toys. I turn it over to the motherland. You wasters get your kicks from immorality; I get mine from service."

"He wants his money," insisted Angel."

"I could just shoot all of you. Our Bangladeshi friend has no objection."

"A British citizen," said Garnet. He looked at Ronnie. "Two British citizens. Remember the Skripal disaster. They forced the general responsible to commit suicide, didn't they?" Ramon squinted at him from behind his round, blue-tinged sunglasses, his bald dome glistening with sweat again, and dug into the cash, pulled out a rubber-banded wad, flicked through it, and flung it at Angel.

"Best you look after it," he said. "I think your boyfriend's about to faint." Angel shoved it into her brassiere. Ramon's gaze swivelled from one to the other. "You've got your tickets booked. Get lost."

Garnet, Angel and Ronnie went down the stairwell and out onto the companionway and down the ladder and then trudged across the beach to where a taxi was waiting.

"Was it worth it, Ronnie?"

"Leave him alone," said Angel.

"I want to retire, again," said Ronnie.

On board, Ramon stared at Smirnov's man, who just shrugged. "You've shown a lot of initiative, pulling this off."

"Thank you."

"Organise the crew. The minibus is still coming for them."

"And then?"

"You're familiar with Asia and you're a competent guy. Who's your official employer?"

"I deserted from the Army during the Afghanistan War."

"You work for the secret service now."

"O.K."

"Only for us."

"O.K."

"And your own fee will be waived. How much do the crew salaries come to?"

"A bit under thirty thousand." Ramon picked out three wads and threw them at him.

"There's thirty. As I'm feeling generous, you can keep the change, but don't cheat them. I don't want any complaints or complications." The other man left the bridge, and Ramon wandered out onto the bridge wing.

Quite satisfying, he thought. He occupied himself thinking up horrific tortures for Smirnov's family.

LXIII

Two weeks earlier, on the ship, outside Bangkok

Alexander raged at Petrov, which was uncharacteristic of him. It was strange how quickly normally cool people with huge self-control lost it with their families. "You idiot," he stammered, finding it hard to spit out the words.

"I love her," insisted Petrov. "I'm sick of you pushing me around." He straightened up, feeling the strength in his massive muscles. "I served the Russian motherland while you were simply ticking boxes and torturing your victims. You're my big brother, but you're a skinny little wimp."

"Half our housing block had her. She has hot pants." Petrov shrugged.

"I don't mind. If I am not there, I am not missing out. Who cares if someone is driving your car while you're not? Really?"

"And you were so stupid as to not let her family know."

"They don't approve of me, even though I am a military hero."

"Military hero? You didn't die. That's all. You're only alive because…"

"So, you admit it. They were going to kill all the enlisted survivors."

"You don't keep her family informed and then her parents think she's gone missing and involve everyone. Those peasants."

"Careful, Alexander. We are peasants, don't forget. Our parents were peasants. The aristocracy were wiped out in the revolution." Alexander looked thoughtful. His face returned to its normal spectral white as the blood left it.

"She has to die."

"What?"

"She has to die, Petrov. Can't you listen? Must I repeat everything. You can find another bed partner. You can't go home, so just pick them up in Pattaya, or, better still, get a Thai one like all the British do."

"Hah, minute I had an Asian woman on my arm, you would explode and say I was an embarrassment to our family."

"I'm not joking."

"You can't kill her. I won't allow it."

"Oh, really?

"I'll kill you, Alexander."

"It will be done before you know anything about it, Petrov. Without me obfuscating everything, you'll be swept up within hours. You're at my mercy, Petrov. You always have been. Even when we were little. And I'm just about sick of protecting you. You're an idiot."

"I won't let you kill her." They stood there, in the engine room of the tanker, glaring at each other, while a Filipino oiler looking at them wondered if they were going to fight.

LXIV

Bangkok

Jeff brought the Chinaman to the basement. The rotund little man was practically salivating, and, as the door clanged shut behind them, his eyes swivelled from the bench with the torture implements to the squirming form of the bound girl. "This worth fifty thousand," he said.

"I told you, you wouldn't be disappointed," replied Jeff. The Englishman went over to the girl and knelt in front of her while she tried, in vain, to slither away. She tried to plaster herself on the wall and Jeff moved his face to within inches of hers. "This man is going to kill you," he said. "Horribly, and there's nothing you can do about that." He turned to look behind him. The Chinaman was playing with a whip. "Shame you're not American. I could have got a fortune for you from him then," he said, turning to face her again. He resisted the temptation to flick his eyes up at the ceiling where the camera lens was hidden in a light fitting. "Do me a favour," he said, leaning back to look down his nose at her, "scream long and loud, and frequently."

There was a roar and the door lock was

vaporised and then Petunia and the Special Victims detective walked in, followed by some more Thai police. "You're under arrest," said the detective.

Jeff slowly stood up. The Chinaman just stood there, looking bemused, the whip hanging limply from his hand. "This part of the entertainment?" he said.

"It is not," said Jeff. "I'm covered by diplomatic immunity."

"Good try," said Petunia.

"I demand to speak to the British Embassy."

"You'd better shut up," said the Special Victims detective as his men slipped handcuffs onto Jeff's wrists. "Where are the cameras?" The Chinaman followed the detective's gaze as he looked over the ceiling.

"There are cameras?" He looked at Jeff. "You bastard. I trusted you."

Some of the Thais cut the girl loose and the detective looked at her. "So much trouble over one girl. First you disappear, then you die, but you don't die. We should never have let Russian tourists into Thailand."

"Yeah," said Jeff. "They ruined it."

"You shut up." The detective pulled Jeff's mobile out of his shirt pocket. "Pin?" he demanded. Jeff reluctantly told him. The detective dialled the last number from which a call had been received and handed the phone to Petunia. When a man answered, she nodded. She held it against her clothing and said, very quietly, to Jeff, "tell him that you need him to come down. Be convincing" She handed him the mobile.

"Yeah, something's happened. You need to come down," he told the man on the end of the line. "Heart attack. Not the girl." Jeff looked at the girl being led out of the basement. "It's the client." He handed the mobile back to Petunia with a shrug. "He's around. Ten minutes."

When the third secretary entered the basement, he gasped, and then stood there while his face reddened as he became infuriated.

LXV

Bangkok

The French Lady sat opposite her Anglo Thai operative on the first floor of the former home of the American silk entrepreneur, on the canal. The operative smiled and then shrugged.

"You betrayed me," she screamed. Her high-pitched voice hurt the man's eardrums. He eyed Chan cracking his fingers.

"No, I didn't," he replied. "You don't deal in snuff." The French Lady's cheeks reddened.

"That's because I don't like it. It brings heat from the authorities." The man shrugged again.

"At least while I was supplying it in conjunction with the British third secretary, it was keeping your competition from getting into the market. Basically, the way I see it, I had your back." The French Lady's face twisted as she tried to work out the logic behind this statement. Chan seemed confused, too.

"I should just kill you now."

"You can do that, but after years of loyal service... And who's going to want to continue working for you if you keep on killing your own operatives?"

"You could lose a hand." At this, Chan shrugged and went over to pick up his machete from where it was leaning against a wall.

"I won't be much use to you with only one hand, will I? Listen, think how difficult I will be to replace. I was brought up in Southampton. Thai mother, British father. I know how to communicate with low-class Brits and I speak fluent Thai. I can drift in and out."

"You've made a fool of me. Petunia knows

about this. That's how I found out"

"She won't tell the Kiwi."

"She already did and what if there is a trial?"

"There won't be any sort of a trial. The British want this buried. The Chinese want it buried. Our own government wants it buried. All employees run side businesses. That's how their employers get to keep salaries low."

"Oh, so now you say it's my fault."

"I didn't say that." The man stood up. "I consider myself reprimanded, O.K.? I'm going now. If you want Chan to shove that machete into my back as I leave, go ahead. I'm still Asian, remember. I know how to accept my fate without whining." The French Lady watched him go and turned to vent her frustration on Chan, but before she could unleash a tide of vitriol, the ape-like man made one of his rare observations.

"You don't win them all," he said.

The third secretary cornered Garnet in Nana plaza. "What did you think you were doing?" he demanded. His irritation was beyond even the abilities of a trained MI6 agent to hide. Garnet shrugged and held out his hands, his palms up.

"You insisted I went after the missing Russian."

"That's all you were supposed to do. Your limited abilities were supposed to get you that far and no further."

"Can't see how it's very fair of you to blame me for your own poor judgement?"

"That was a British operation."

"Oh, yeah? A stolen ship?"

"You know I'm referring to the girl and the..."

"Yeah, yeah. A bit of cover for you. You were running a side business and you probably found out they were on to you and saw a way to hide everything behind some spurious operation. There were pools of blood in that basement, dried blood. I don't think all the victims were part of legitimate blackmail plots. Anyway, you still had intent, didn't you? That Chinese isn't off the hook."

"Once Petunia got the Thais involved, we had to give him up."

"All's fair in love and war. If you fail, try, try again. Not sending you home, are they? We've got used to you around here and your special brand of incompetence." The third secretary looked as if he wanted to throttle Garnet. He managed to control himself, however, just barely, and turned and strode off, his Mackintosh flapping around his ankles. "I should get one of them," Garnet shouted after him. "Perfect for the rainy season."

The third secretary consoled himself with a beer in the Reichstag. The conversation with the home office hadn't gone well. They'd been pretty suspicious. Jeff, luckily, had been set free in order to avoid any further embarrassment, and disappeared, probably to Cambodia, but there had been sharp questions. "Why hadn't he cleared it with London first?" for a start. Typical. They were so keen to avoid responsibility that they never O.Kay'd anything formally and then if you did something and it didn't work out... But if you just never did anything then they accused you of slacking. Public school gits, he thought. He decided to have one more try with the ambassador.

The ambassador's secretary knew better than to try to deny him access and just watched from behind her steel-framed spectacles as he pushed open the door to the ambassador's office. The ambassador was lying naked, face down, on a massage table and a muscular Thai was working him over. "Lower, Benny," said the ambassador, but not too low. I know you, you naughty boy." The third secretary bit his lip again. He was in danger of chewing it off.

"Garnet," he said.

"Oh, not him again."

"Yeah, him."

"Yeah, him. Your un-dulcet tones and street lingo are tiring, Third Secretary. I'm not quite the uninformed moron whom you seem to believe I am. You're lucky that you're not in jail and that you still have a job."

"It was a legitimate operation, for Queen and country."

"Only a moron, and I repeat, I am not a moron, would believe that this was the first girl who went through your system, and you sold them and pocketed the cash which I am sure is in some Cayman Islands bank account and H.M. Government could find it if it was motivated to, which, again, luckily for you, it is not. Do leave me alone. Benny is about to work on my tender bits and pieces and he's an artist so shouldn't be subjected to any distractions." The third secretary gave up and left.

LXVI

A maximum-security prison Siberia

Roman led Smirnov's naked wife along the catwalk over the open-barred tops of the cells. Her wrists were bound, more from a desire on Roman and the guards' part to avoid any unnecessary scratches, than due to a serious belief that she could cause mischief. Roman had expected outrage, which was the norm among victims who had previously considered themselves to be occupying positions of privilege, but she was going for bravery. If he weren't such a seasoned tormentor, he might have believed it to be more than the little charade it was.

He stopped, abruptly, and turned to face her. He admired her body. The birth of a single child certainly hadn't marked it. It looked, from the condition of her breasts, as though she'd bottle fed him. "We have reached your destination," he said.

"What?" she stammered. Ramon looked down through the bars of the cell above which they were standing.

"These are the worst of the worst," he said. "Not political prisoners, not by a long way. You might almost call them professional rapists, though they prefer to think of themselves as assassins and the like. Look at them." Her eyes followed his finger and she found herself gazing upon the half-naked, hulking forms of eight vicious-looking thugs who were staring up at her. "They don't jeer," said Roman. "Talking is banned. It brings very serious punishments. But they are fascinated."

"You brought me here so that they could stare at me?" Roman laughed and signalled the jailor to move into action. The man unclasped a bundle of keys and leapt off the catwalk onto the bars over the top of the cell, and then he opened a lock and flung open a horizontal gate.

"You're a gift to them," said Roman. "Don't worry, they won't kill you. Well, not unless you haemorrhage. They won't kill you intentionally."

"Wait," pleaded the woman. Roman scoffed.

"Wait for what? Don't go down there with any delusions that this isn't justice. Your husband, that bastard, handed over a Russian girl to be tortured to death. He did it for cash. There wasn't even a semblance of justice involved as there is in this." She glanced down at the waiting criminals again. One of them was salivating.

"This is not justice. It wasn't I."

"You lived off Alexander's criminal earnings. Did you ever ask him how he could afford your mink on a Russian Government salary?" He raised his eyebrows, quizzically. "Didn't think so." He dropped his voice to a whisper. "One of them is known to be a soft touch. If you cry, it might help you." He nodded at the guard and the guard swooped her up.

"My son?" she said.

"What about him?"

"Will you hurt him?" Roman looked offended.

"Certainly not," he said. "We are not monsters." Then he nodded at the guard again and the guard flung her over the catwalk and through the opening in the top of the cage and she fell into the waiting arms of the monsters below. Soon, she was buried beneath slabs of muscle and they could only be sure she was still alive and squirming owing to her shrieks.

LXVII

Siberia

Smirnov's child sat in the tent which belonged to the indigenous family in the remote part of Siberia which had been told to adopt him. He looked at the pot of raw meat in the centre of the tent and at his new brothers and sisters, who were happily chomping down on some, their rosy cheeks seeming to signify a general sense of happiness. He had his bag of toy cars in front of him. The bald man with the spectacles had been keen to see that he took them with him. The boy had mistakenly assumed this had been an act of kindness, but Roman had simply wanted him to remember the life which he had lost. Actually, soon, Smirnov's son would probably find himself living in another ugly high-rise, very similar to the ugly high-rise building in Moscow in which his father had bought the very expensive apartment which had been, until very recently, the family home. Russia's oil and gas companies were busily ruining the tribal lands and the native community would be shuffled off into some state housing in an area in which investigative reporters never intruded. Such was life.

The boy's new father leant across and nudged

him, a broad smile upon his face, urging him to eat, and the little boy picked out a piece and bit into the flesh. To his surprise, it actually tasted nicer that the burgers at the American restaurant chain to which Smirnov had taken them regularly in order to let everyone know he could afford to.

He smiled back at his adoptive father. This new life was going to be a lot more fun than sitting in that stuffy old apartment with his mother, watching her preen herself.

LXVIII

Bangkok

Sergey puffed on one of his cheap cigarettes and quaffed a beer outside the Union Jack. Garnet looked away and took a drag on his own cigarette. "You're going to kill yourself, droog," he said, out of the side of his mouth.

"What?"

"You're drinking and smoking yourself into an early grave, plus your idea of a sensible diet is probably fat boiled up, mixed with ketchup and called borscht."

"That is not an accurate description of borscht."

"Plus, your stress levels."

"I will be sent to the teaching hospital in St Petersburg if I have a heart attack."

"You've got to make it there. The only way you'll be travelling back to mother Russia if you get a heart attack, will be in an Aeroflot cargo compartment inside a coffin. Don't sulk. I'm grateful for you for bringing in Roman."

"You should have listened to me."

"I should."

"I told you not to get involved. You have upset

your own intelligence operative."

"By stopping him sacrificing a Russian girl? I should have thought you'd be grateful."

"She is just a bitch."

"And stopping him getting full blackmail material on a Chinese defence company official? You should be grateful for that, too."

"Hmmm."

"My friend might have been killed if I weren't involved," mused Garnet. "Why did you really give up Smirnov?"

"You gave him up."

"You already knew, didn't you? Was it because he wouldn't cut you in?"

"He was an idiot. Stealing ships. Idiot. Are you a big mouth?"

"Only when I'm drunk."

"One of my former sailing companions on LPG ships was cheated by Smirnov."

"But you didn't win anything out of this. Roman gets the credit. Revenge... What is that?"

"You are not Russian. You don't understand."

"What did they do with Smirnov's wife?"

"She will have a good time, before she dies."

"And his son?"

"Gone to a better place." Garnet raised his eyebrows. "Moscow is a disaster. Full of immigrants. Believe me, he will be happier where he is, though I doubt that was the state's intention."

"In England 'gone to a better place' means 'died'."

"In Russia, it simply means 'gone to a better place'.

"And Smirnov's brother? Gobbing off about the Kursk? Is that why Ramon wanted him gone?" Sergey snorted with derision.

"Even some grandmother in a remote Siberian village knows the true story of the Kursk. Putin did the right thing. No one wants war with the U.S. He was involved with the Losharik. Even the Americans don't want that submarine disaster talked about. 'Planetary catastrophe'? It could have been."

"So, who owes whom a favour?"

"You want to turn me down for a favour when I ask for one, then go ahead. I do not advise it."

"O.K., droog. Your foreign fan club awaits you inside this part of a foreign dump which will be forever England."

"Hah, you love Bangkok."

"I do. Don't we all?"

"Half the people inside there would kill themselves if they were forced to move back to Britain." Garnet slapped his arm around Sergey's wall of muscle.

"More than half, droog."

LXIX

Ruby stomped on board, causing James's smile to change from one of service-minded welcome to a fixed grin as he took in her heels stomping along the teak of the passeurelle. Her Chanel handbag hung from her right-hand like a club with which she was looking to beat him. "Captain," she hissed, "and I hope he is not in the strip clubs."

"Oh, he's on board," replied James, happily. He didn't think he could have coped with her full-on rage if their portly leader had been in Suzie Wong's. He went inside and found the captain flicking through a Taschen book of artistic nudes. "Kim Jong Ding Dong's sister is here to see you," he told him. The captain flipped the book shut and followed him out onto the aft deck. He flushed once he'd taken in the anger evident in her facial expression.

"Ruby," he said.

"Ha. If I were a man, you would not use my first name."

"I only use your first name as a kind of term of endearment."

"Shut up, you foolish little man."

"Now you listen..." Ruby affected patience while the captain simply became more and more flustered.

"I'm listening." The captain wagged his finger.

"Aha," he said.

"Aha what?"

"Where's your technical superintendent? So-called technical superintendent, I might add in clarification. Doesn't even have a commercial ship's engineer's licence or a degree, apart from, possibly, something in Caterpillar digger maintenance from the University of Wagga Wagga."

"I will not tolerate your insolence."

"I am the master of this vessel. You're just some jumped-up M.B.A. woman from Guangzhou or whatever the BBC has decided Canton should be called this week." James winced and looked off to the side, suddenly finding the sight of the hookers swanning around in skimpy bikinis on the adjacent yacht irresistible despite his almost Christian-like abhorrence of commercial sex.

"You are a servant of our management company."

"I am not. I am a servant of our owner and I've been running this boat for fourteen years, without your help. What do you want?"

"I am sick of you shirking your responsibilities. How dare you complain that our technical superintendent ran away?" The captain was outraged.

"He did! Typical. That's what Australians do. Same with their crew. Someone offers them a little bit more, they're gone, doesn't matter what training courses etc. the boat paid for. 'I have to think of myself'." He was quoting some obstreperous stewardess whom they'd hired during an experimental period when they'd tried bringing on white interior staff which had proven to be a disaster.

"What happened to him?"

"How the hell should I know."

"He disappeared while he was on your boat." The captain put his hands on his hips and stuck his belly out in defiance.

"I don't know. Started up a meth lab?" he suggested. "Struck me as the type. Have you tried the police?"

"They don't want to get involved."

"Can't say I blame them. One more Aussie whom no one liked disappears and..."

"I will not tolerate this. I shall recommend to the owner that he fires you." The injustice roiled the captain. Ruby turned to leave. She paused and looked over her shoulder at him. "Your owner is buying a bigger boat, you know, and you aren't qualified to drive it."

"I shall go with this boat to its new owner."

"I shall see that you don't." She stomped back down the passeurelle.

"And take your shoes off next time before you come on board," shouted the captain. He turned to James.

"She does look a bit like her," he said.

"Like whom?"

"Kim of North Korea's sister. Hmmm," continued the captain, thoughtfully. "I think we should swop them. I can't believe that woman's more evil than Ruby."

"I wonder where Johnno went."

"Who cares. Went back to the Philippines building a hut for his umpteenth Filipina wife and got eaten by one of those native tribes in their loin cloths. If that happened, they did us a favour. I'd like to buy their chief a drink in Suzie Wong's. I want to get back to my reading."

"To your artistic nudes."

"Insolent... Hmmm. Now I sound like her."

LXX

Garnet hung over the balcony of their hotel in Phuket and was startled when his mobile rang and displayed a U.K. number. He answered the call. As soon as the woman on the other end of the line started speaking, he recognised the voice. You bastard, Andre, he thought, you didn't even tell her. He made a tentative effort at speaking, but then fell silent. He wondered if he should just hang up, but he was finding it more and more difficult over the years to look at himself in the mirror. Cowardice in the face of someone who was going to physically harm you if he could was one thing, but hanging up on this woman would just be shameful.

"Did you find him?" she repeated.

"Your husband found himself involved in something bordering on the illegal," said Garnet. What am I doing, he asked himself. It wasn't bordering on illegal; it was piracy. "He didn't want to do it and tried to back out," he continued. "It's possible he'd been forced into doing what he was doing. It was nothing sordid. I can't tell you too much; it's very sensitive, but it was nothing sordid."

"He won't be coming home?" Garnet had told Andre that the body fished out of the river might have been the engineer, but had never informed him when the positive I.D. came though.

"I'm sorry. I don't think so. He's disappeared. We have reason to believe..." There was a sob. "I'm sorry," he said. He didn't think it was necessary to refer to the bloated corpse that might not have even been him. After all, they didn't do a DNA test. "There were no women involved," he added, and the woman screeched with emotional pain. Garnet wanted to kick himself. He was basically autistic when it came to judging women's emotions and how to deal with them

"Thank you, Mr Garnet," said the woman. "You've been so kind." Then she did hang up. Garnet slumped and then straightened up. Life goes on, he thought. He dealt in tragedy every day, but the victims were normally fools or sexual deviants or both. This woman...

LXXI

Bangkok

Ronnie and Angel sat in the car dealers, the dealer swinging his swivel chair from side to side as he looked first at one of them and then at the other. The scarlet, second-hand Mazda sports car, sat gleaming on the forecourt, receiving a final polish from the street kid employed occasionally for this sort of odd job. The dealer took a risk and passed the keys over to Ronnie and received a full-on glare from an indignant ladyboy who snatched them away. "No offence," said the dealer, politely. He tried to smile his way out of it but this operation met with abject failure. Angel pushed her own swivel chair round with her long legs, climbed out of it, raised herself to her full, intimidating height and marched out onto the forecourt, Ronnie trailing her. She swept the boy aside, opened the driver's door and got in and started up the little car's engine. Ronnie rushing round and clambering in on the other side, worried he might be left behind.

As they were leaving the forecourt, someone slapped the boot. Angel jumped out of the car, ready to stick a stiletto into the miscreant and then there were cries of joy and hugs. Ronnie remained in the car, idly looking at the truck which they were holding up. The truck driver beeped his horn and Ronnie shrugged. Then Angel clambered back in, a pair of skinny, olive legs appeared between them and Ronnie turned his head to find another ladyboy was sitting on the boot. He recognised her: a good friend of Angel's

Angel and her friend tried having a conversation but with the traffic noise and the wind it was impossible so they pulled up in front of a ladyboy-friendly café and went inside.

While they all sipped frappuccinos, there was some conversation going on in Thai between the two girls, which grew more and more acrimonious.

"Ladies," whispered Ronnie, trying to quieten things down. Angel hissed at him. Then she decided to involve him.

"One of our friends was murdered," she said, "a very good friend of mine. Raped and killed."

"Happens every day, doesn't it?"

"By a white man."

"Again, happens every day, doesn't it?"

"There are rumours."

"And?" Ronnie wasn't really interested, but went along. He wanted to be, or, at least, seem to be, supportive.

"There were Russians involved."

"There are a million Russians here."

"And a ship's engineer. The guy whom you…"

"How do these things leak out?"

"They just do."

"The ladyboy union will deal with it."

"I am in the ladyboy union."

"Of course, you are, but…"

"But what?"

"Let someone else deal with it."

"Raped, Ronnie."

"What's the difference. You get a crumpled bit of paper that someone will exchange a McDonald's for if you're not, that's all." Angel slapped him. "The metoo movement arrives in ladyboyland," mused Ronald. The slap hadn't even caused his cheek to redden. His veins were too collapsed for the blood to flow freely enough. "Angel, I don't want you to go to Klong Prem." The other ladyboy said something.

"I am the best fighter and the toughest," Angel summarised.

"He's just another Russian. Kill him and there's still a million more. Anyway, maybe the one (he flicked his eyes at the other ladyboy) who met his demise in the land of the Chapati did it. You don't know."

"Anyway, the one left behind must pay. No ladyboy death will go unavenged." Ronnie laughed. "What!"

"I was just thinking: sounds like a line from a Marvel Comic or something. Imagine that: a ladyboy superhero. Who would play him, do you think? I mean play her? Matt Damon? Needs to be someone who could pass."

"Don't joke, Ronnie."

"Who's joking. Could be millions in this." There was some more rapid Thai and then the other ladyboy left. "Listen, Angel, we have the car of your dreams. I'm still raking it in ripping off pool players who overrate themselves. You can always sell your bottom. We don't need any stress, do we?"

"Ronnie, you don't understand."

"Think of your mother. Think of your mother in the event that you get caught. Farm it out. Someone does the ladyboy movement a favour; later on, the ladyboy union does him a favour."

"Raped and killed, "Ronnie.

"So, a gay male assassin. Must be some. I've known a few types in the merchant navy who would have been up for something like that. But you need a professional."

"It is a personal thing, Ronnie."

"Angel."

"Didn't I just save your life? Answer the question."

"Quite possibly," said Ronnie, sadly. Angel jabbed at the Formica tabletop with her stiletto until the café owner hissed at her. "I'll…"

"I don't need the details, Angel."

"You don't get a say in this."

"Don't worry, I'll join in the monkey visits."

"You think you're safe because you don't

think we'll be able to find him. The ladyboy union has ten thousand spies." Ronnie sipped his frothy coffee, his upper lip getting coated in foam.

"Whatever you want, Angel. I'm too tired to spend another fruitless half hour trying to dissuade you. Kill him. Don't rape him, though. That makes you the same as him."

In Pattaya, Smirnov's former accomplice lay back in his hotel bed receiving oral sex from two teenage girls, blissfully unaware that he was doomed.

LXXII

Phuket

Garnet lay on his Union Jack towel on the sand at Patong. Prudence, in her nice designer, upper-middle-class bikini looked over at him. She raised her Chanel sunglasses. "I wish you wouldn't bring that to the beach; it's so embarrassing. You're not even patriotic."

"I don't like people to think I'm Australian." Garnet looked her over. "You don't look bad for a bird approaching middle-age," he said.

"Lucky that I'm immune to your offensive observations," replied Prudence. "Don't bother with any self-sabotage, Garnet. I know that this isn't going to lead to my taking a second stroll up the aisle. There's no need to be 'unintentionally' nasty and then make out you don't understand how you ruined everything. Just be happy to be with me. That's all I want."

"Simpler when women only want money."

"You're doing it again." Garnet laughed. "You want me to think you're an old whoremonger, but I know you only sleep with one strip club girl and that you're in love with her."

"I am not."

"But can't admit it." A Scandinavian boy with a golden tan and wavy blond hair went by and Garnet noticed Prudence's gaze following him, but said nothing. "What shall we do tomorrow?" Garnet thought about this.

"Must be some elephant sanctuary or something. The shopping mall's terrible."

"Well it's not Siam Paragon. I'm serious, Garnet."

"What? We're only talking about holiday pastimes." She punched him on the arm, playfully.

"Jill?"

"Ah. Jill." Garnet lay back in the sand, having been perched with his chin resting on his elbow. "I don't think I've ever had a woman jealous over me before."

"You think I'm jealous? O.K. I am. What do you think about Jill, seriously?"

"She's just a whore."

William Gilbert, 2020

www.ingramcontent.com/pod-product-compliance
Lightning Source LLC
Chambersburg PA
CBHW071442150726
48000CB00013B/371